OPERATOR 5:
THE DAY OF THE DAMNED

SECRET SERVICE OPERATOR #5™
AMERICA'S UNDERCOVER ACE

THE DAY OF
THE DAMNED

By Curtis Steele

POPULAR PUBLICATIONS • 2024

CHAPTER 1
DATE WITH DEATH

TWO TELEGRAPH messages lay on the desk of the manager of the Acme Exporting Company—two short, seemingly ordinary telegrams. Yet as the manager stared at them with keen blue eyes, his brow wrinkled in a frown and his fingertips tapped thoughtfully on the arms of his chair. One message was from New Orleans, the other from Santa Fe; one from a girl reporter, the other from a state governor. And Jimmy Christopher sensed that both messages vitally concerned the safety of the United States.

That New Orleans telegram had come from Diane Elliot. On scores of occasions, she had served him and her country with steadfast courage. Her quick intelligence had made her his most valued assistant. Now that the Purple Wars were a thing of the past, and the threat of European invasion through Canada had been dissipated, Diane had returned to her pre-war calling. She was traveling with Triumvir Joab Burley's party as an ace reporter for a news syndicate.

It was at Jimmy Christopher's suggestion that she had gone after that assignment. He wanted a confidential report on the activities of the barn-storming Triumvir who left the cares of state to his two companions while he toured the country in a round of speeches and dinners. Joab Burley, it seemed, had not outgrown the early training that had made him a power in New

1

York politics. His smiling face was photographed in city after city, his hands gesticulating in vehement oratory or stretched out for double-barreled handshakes to the surrounding crowds.

If Burley's activity meant nothing more than that, there was no cause for concern. But disturbing rumors had drifted back

Down from the sky rained the disease-infected bodies of the plague-dead!

to the business office that was a blind for the New York headquarters of the man America knew as Operator 5.

"Thanks for your suggestion," ran this message of Diane's. "Following your lead should give us a front-page feature."

A front-page feature? That meant trouble—that Joab Burley was engaged in something that would prove sensational when revealed. Jimmy Christopher's clean-cut face clouded, his frown deepening. Then his eyes shifted to the second message.

It had come from Hugh Delcourt, former mayor of Santa Fe and now governor of New Mexico—and also one of Operator 5's most trusted agents in the Southwest. Like Diane's, Delcourt's message was brief, prosaic.

"Valuable shipment will arrive in New York on the Southern Pacific liner *Tremont* on the twentieth," it read. "Kindly be prepared for prompt handling."

Prompt handling—that meant more trouble; something that would require immediate attention. The twentieth—that was today. Jimmy glanced at the clock. It was after ten, and the *Tremont* should dock shortly after noon. The messenger should arrive by one or two. But at that moment a secretary appeared at the private office door.

"A radio message from the *Tremont,*" he announced.

"Samples require immediate delivery," that wireless read. "Please meet at pier with car. John Borden."

Operator 5's eyes narrowed the moment he glimpsed that signature. His alert, youthful face became sharper, as his nerves tingled with suppressed excitement. There was no John Borden in the secret service. The name was code—a warning that the

4

operative who employed it knew that death was closing in on him!

THAT DESPAIRING call for help Jimmy Christopher answered promptly. He was on hand at the Southern Pacific pier before the *Tremont* landed. All his plans were made. He had a car waiting to speed the newly arrived messenger to safety, alert undercover men posted at various points of vantage. But when the gangplanks were lowered and the passengers streamed ashore, he looked in vain for the man from Santa Fe. Carefully, he scrutinized every face in the passing throng, yet none was familiar.

Already, he had assembled in his mind all those who possibly might be coming from Hugh Delcourt. None of them had appeared, and the crowd was already thinning out. Then he noticed that an elderly man with a short gray beard was coming in his direction. Something about the man's stride, about the way he headed for Jimmy, made his intention unmistakable… but he got no closer than within twenty feet of his objective.

Suddenly, the metal-roofed pier rang with the crackling chatter of machine-gun fire. A blast of flame and lead cut recklessly into the thinning crowd, snuffed the buzz of conversation with a hushed silence that gave way to shrieks of terror and screams of agony!

Jimmy saw the old fellow go down. He glimpsed the tommy-gun muzzle swinging in his own direction, just in time to fling himself to one side. One of the slugs caught him in the shoulder, but his body was thrusting out of the line of fire. And then his own automatic was in his hand, blazing away at two dark-complexioned men now glaring at him with murderous eyes.

His bullet caught one of them, flung him backward. Jimmy saw him go down, then leap back onto his feet, blood already soaking the front of his shirt and coat—but at that instant a blue-uniformed pier guard sprang into action. His arm swept up and knocked the tommy-gun out of the other killer's hands, just as it recommenced to spout. For a moment, he and the fellow were trading blows. Then both of the assassins were fleeing, ducking pell-mell through the terrified throng, with the guard in hot pursuit.

It had all taken place in a fraction of a second. Before Jimmy could fire a second time, the guard had been in the way—and then his targets were lost in the crowd. Even before he reached the street, he saw a car leap away from the curb, heard its motor roar as it darted off at top speed with the fugitives.

To attempt to pick up their trail would be a waste of time. Regretfully, Jimmy turned and walked back to where the old man had fallen. He still lay there on the wooden floor—and a glance at his ashen face, at the row of bullet-holes that seamed his chest, pronounced him dead.

A young doctor was kneeling beside the corpse. Getting to his feet, when he looked up into Jimmy's face, he flashed quick recognition. "He's dead—killed instantly. It's a better job than they did on board."

Something about that white face had caught Jimmy Christopher's attention. Quickly, he knelt beside the corpse, peered closely at the still features. He discovered that, instead of being an old man, the victim was young—David, the twenty-five-year-old son of Hugh Delcourt!

"You are bleeding, yourself," the physician said, as he bent over Jimmy. "That shoulder wound may be bad. Better let me attend to it, before there is chance of infection."

Before Jimmy could protest, he was helping him out of his coat, cutting away the bullet-ripped shirt sleeve, washing the wound with disinfectant and dressing it. All the while, his eyes darted surreptitious, knowing glances at Jimmy's face.

"What was that you said about something that happened on the boat?" Jimmy remembered suddenly.

"They tried to kill him one night on deck. It must have been the same pair, though he made no attempt to describe them," the doctor spoke low-voiced, as he worked. "They tried knives that time—gave him three nasty wounds before he managed to get away from them. I found him reeling across the deck, hardly able to stand on his feet. I dressed the wounds for him. That was when I discovered that he wasn't just what he seemed to be. He made no attempt to explain his masquerade—swore me to secrecy about it."

So that was the reason for the last-minute radiogram, for the desperate call for help! Young Delcourt had known that his identity had been discovered, that death hung over him. He had met it there on the pier, an unknown hero whose sacrifice for his country would go unsung and un-remembered—except by Operator 5 and a few of his intimates who knew that only by eternal vigilance and eternal sacrifice like this could the freedom of the Republic be preserved....

"I don't know what this is all about, but I *want* to know," the young physician was saying. "I have seen enough to make me curious, and to make me want to take a hand—especially since I recognized you, sir. Operator 5 has been my hero for years—the man I would rather work with than anyone else in the world. My name is Norman King. I'm a physician, from Dallas, Texas—I know this may seem a queer ambition for a doctor—but I don't see why medicine should not come in handy in your work." King's tone was earnest, his words almost pleading.

When Jimmy looked into the man's gray eyes, they were excited, sparkling with anticipation. He might have the makings of a recruit for that little band of loyal undercover workers whose number was constantly being thinned by the swift rush of death. In any case, Jimmy wanted to talk with him further, and so took him back to the Acme office.

"After ten years of warfare I have been through, I find it pretty hard to settle down," the young medico availed himself of the opportunity for further explanation. "I am here in New York to do some research work, but I have very little enthusiasm for it. I don't want to play around with cultures and guinea pigs when men are dying like that fellow on the pier. He did a man's job—and that's what I want to do. I want to tie up with the secret service if they can use me. Besides being a physician—"

His argument was cut short by the telephone bell, and Jimmy Christopher reached for the instrument.

"Mr. Christopher," a male voice came guardedly over the wire. "This is you, Mr. Christopher—Operator 5? This is one of the Southern Pacific pier guards speaking. I was there when they tried to kill you a little while ago, and I trailed them. I have them both; the one you shot—he's dead now—and his partner!"

The pier guard who had saved his life! And he had trailed the killers—had captured one of them alive! Jimmy Christopher's pulses leaped, as he visioned an opportunity to make the killer talk, to make him reveal what lay behind that ruthless murder.

"Where are you, man?" he barked into the phone; but the guard was already giving the address of a midtown apartment building. Jimmy jotted it down and grabbed for his hat.

"You've been in this thing so far—you might as well see the rest of it," he called in an afterthought to Norman King, as he strode lithely to the door, his wide-shouldered, narrow-hipped body moving with the smooth rhythm of an athlete.

But the doctor was already at his side, keeping brisk step with him, anxious not to be left behind.

A TAXICAB sped them uptown, and King waited impatiently while Jimmy paid the driver. Eagerly, King started into the lobby—only to be suddenly brushed aside and sent spinning across the entranceway, as Jimmy's automatic leaped into his hand and blazed through the inner doorway.

The roar of that shot echoed another from across the lobby, and a bullet smashed into the wall just where King had been standing. Once more Jimmy Christopher's gun barked. But now there was no response. After a wary moment, he catfooted into the building and crouched over the sprawled figure of a man whose dark-skinned face was covered with blood.

A Spaniard or a Mexican, evidently—but death had sealed the lips of the would-be ambusher.

Jimmy swung himself to one side, automatic in his hand!

Quickly, Jimmy led the way upstairs to the apartment the pier guard had designated. The door was closed but unlocked. Cautiously, he opened it and listened, caught a half-moan from within. Gun ready, he padded across the tiny foyer and into a disordered living-room. The blue-uniformed pier guard was just picking himself up from the floor.

"I thought I had him tied up," he mumbled dazedly, as his fingers gingerly felt a lump rapidly swelling on the back of his head. "I turned my back a minute—and I must have seen a thousand stars. I don't see how he could have gotten loose, how he got out of that chair—"

But Jimmy Christopher was kneeling beside a corpse that lay on the floor. This man, like the one in the lobby, was dark-skinned and had the broad, flat features of a Mexican Indian.

"They were Mexes—both of them," the discomfited guard volunteered. "I couldn't get the live fellow to talk—but I know Mexicans when I see them. I come from down that way myself, from New Mexico."

As he listened, Jimmy was going over the room—fingering the sparse contents of a writing desk, leafing through several sheets of paper with notations in English and Spanish. Copies of the telegram Hugh Delcourt had sent him and also of the radiogram from the *Tremont!* So these two killers were not the ones who had attacked young Delcourt on the boat, They were fellow-plotters, stationed here in New York and kept fully apprised of their victim's progress. They had known that Operator 5 could be reached at the Acme Exporting office and that he would be down to meet the boat!

"That's how I knew where to call you." The pier guard seemed to read his thoughts. "I read through those papers—and then I knew it was Operator 5 they tried to kill. My name is Dalbert Eastman, sir. You never heard of me, but I saw you put an end to the Blaintree rebellion. I saw you lick Corvallo and Godkin, east of Santa Fe. I couldn't get away from home then—my folks thought I was too young. But I wanted to come north and see if I couldn't tie up with the secret service."

Like Norman King's his face was now alight with enthusiasm and he pleaded eagerly.

"This wasn't so good—letting that fellow get away," he admitted ruefully, "but I *did* manage to trail them here and get into the place. I was too anxious, that's why he slipped out of my hands. But it won't ever happen to me again. I don't know what this trouble is all about, Operator 5—but it looks as if it's made to order for me. Those fellows were both Mexicans. That looks like trouble in the Southwest—and I know the Mexican border like I know my own backyard. Give me a chance to show you what I can do."

His words rushed on, but that phrase, "trouble in the Southwest," was burned in Jimmy Christopher's brain. For weeks his eyes had been turning uneasily toward the Rio Grande, his ears attuned to catch the faintest rumble from across the border. And now he knew that his misgivings had not been without foundation.

There was trouble brewing in Mexico—trouble that threatened to sweep north in a steel-crested tidal wave!

Hugh Delcourt's ominous secrecy, and now his son's death,

confirmed the fears that had been preying on Operator 5 day and night. America was in danger, and his place was down there where the storm would break. But first he would have to stop at Washington to confer with Triumvir Warren.

For a moment, he regarded Norman King and Dalbert Eastman doubtfully, and then he made up his mind. Perhaps he would be able to find a use for one or the other of them. But, in any case, he wanted to be able to keep an eye on both of them— and the best way to be able to do that was to take them along!

CHAPTER 2
THE YELLOW TIDE RISES

THE SECOND White House, Washington had dubbed the simple white colonial residence on Pennsylvania Avenue where Andrew Warren made his home. In actuality, it was the equivalent of the executive mansion of pre-war Presidents—for, while America had three rulers under the Triumvirate, it was Warren who shouldered the tremendous weight of administerial duties and responsibility for the rebuilding nation.

As soon as he had registered at a hotel in the capital city, and arranged to meet Eastman and King there later in the day, Jimmy Christopher hurried to report to his chief. His mind was busily occupied with the words that absorbed it, as he walked up the broad stone steps—so absorbed that he almost collided head-on with Japan's Ambassador Ito Okatura.

"So sorry—so sorry." The Oriental bowed low in apology as

he drew back. "It was I who was in your way—I must be more careful."

Suave and smiling, the bland little statesman met the near collision as he met everything else—as if it was a carefully arranged part of his program. The polite words clipped from his lips, as if they had been memorized and held ready for the cue to release them; and in the depths of his dark, inscrutable eyes laughter seemed to dance.

Jubilant laughter, Jimmy would have sworn. Again he had that feeling that Okatura was chuckling inwardly—that his words had a carefully calculated double meaning. Okatura gave the impression of a man who was sitting back and watching with huge enjoyment the unfolding of a drama, to which he held the key....

Jimmy Christopher was not the only one who experienced that vague uneasiness. The moment he was ushered into Triumvir Warren's presence, he saw that the gray-haired old fighter was a badly worried man. Warren's handsome, distinguished face was grave, and his troubled eyes seemed to be staring into the far distance, as if they would see beyond the limits of mortal vision.

"Even had I not just bumped into him, I would have known that Ito Okatura had just been in to see you," Jimmy greeted, as Warren rose to shake his hand, warmly. "He has left his stamp on you, sir."

"I know—I know." The Triumvir sank back into his chair. "Perhaps I am over-suspicious, over-prone to worry since our narrow escape from Franz Schnabel's plotting—but I can't feel at ease. As usual, Ambassador Okatura just gave me his profound assurance that Japan has none but the warmest feelings for the United States. To hear him talk, the Mikado would sooner wreck his empire than do anything to endanger our friendship. But I can't believe him, Jimmy. I can't forget that Japan was all ready to step in and share in the partition of the American continent."

Six months before, America had passed through its greatest crisis since the death of Emperor Rudolph and the expulsion of the Purple invaders who had almost annihilated the nation. Struggling heroically to rebuild on the ruins the Purple armies had left in their wake, the almost helpless country had been a tempting prize to the eyes of Europe's dictators. Germany's Reichsfuehrer, Franz Schnabel, had been unable to resist that temptation and had plotted to seize and subjugate the entire American continent, with the aid of Italy and Japan— had schemed to divide it with his allies and eventually convert it all into a German colony. Through the efforts of Operator 5 and a gallant band of secret operatives, Schnabel's intention to use Italy as a cat's-paw had been revealed and his treacherous plotting had failed. After the collapse of the Italian-German invasion, Japan, the third member of the pact, had disclaimed all connection with the pillaging scheme.

Great Britain, at the time of the unsuccessful invasion, had been too engrossed at home to send help to America. However, the British Asiatic fleet had been patrolling the Pacific, on the watch for Japanese invaders setting out for the American coast—and, in Jimmy Christopher's opinion, it was that vigilance which had made the Japanese hesitate until they learned that their intended allies had failed.

Since that time, the British fleet had maintained its supervision of the Pacific, had patrolled the entire North American coast from the Aleutian Islands to Panamá. The only Japanese they had encountered were immigrants—Japanese farmers, flocking to Mexico at the invitation of President Miguel Toledaro.

It was this wave of Japanese immigration that had been worrying America—particularly as it was well known that Toledaro was hostilely anti-American and deliberately over-friendly with the Japanese Government.

"I HAVE reports here—" Triumvir Warren nodded toward the papers piled high on his desk—"that indicate that more than a hundred thousand Japanese men and women have landed at Mexican ports during the past six months. Farmers and their wives, ostensibly—but General Ferrara is certain that those farmers are actually soldiers being imported for an invasion across the Rio Grande." He frowned.

"On the other hand—" he picked up a typewritten sheet and scanned it thoughtfully—"here is a report from one of your men stationed at Acapulco that seems to belie the general. Your man has checked and verified that every Jap is bringing his wife with him, besides his household goods and farm machinery. He saw one of those cases drop out of the sling that was hoisting it overside, and break open on the dock—saw plows, harrows and innocent farm utensils spill out of it. That would seem to indicate that these immigrants are nothing more than the simple tillers of the soil they pretend to be."

And yet Jimmy Christopher knew that Warren was not convinced; knew just what was in the back of his mind.

There was more than this yellow tide to arouse apprehension. During the past few months, Mexican oil had gone completely out of the world market—except for Japan. The rest was being consumed at home—a tremendous quantity for such a purpose.

"Mexico has no industries capable of utilizing that much fuel," General Ferrara had pointed out. "That means the oil is not being used; it is being stored—set aside for military use in the near future. When the Japanese are ready to launch their invasion, they will need petroleum in great quantities—and Toledaro will have it there ready for them."

Ferrara was so concerned with what he was confident would be an early invasion that he had turned his attention from the Canadian border to the Southwest. Leaving his assistants in charge of the well nigh impregnable Ferrara Line, which now guarded America from the Great Lakes to Vancouver, he had hastened to the Mexican border and was now organizing its defense—was trying to erect a similar barrier from the Pacific to the Gulf of Mexico.

That was a prodigious undertaking—one which would take many months to complete—and Ferrara was sure that he had no more than days in which to prepare for the yellow flood….

The only member of the Triumvirate who did no worrying was rotund, ruddy-faced Joab Burley. He, too, was in the South—on one of the periodic "pepping up" tours which seemed to take him to the Southern states whenever the Northern weather became inclement.

"There are two reasons why I am here, sir," Jimmy explained. "One is Joab Burley—has he had anything worth while to report?"

"Nothing more than the excellence of Southern cuisine and the wonderful reception he is receiving," Andrew Warren sighed. "You have noticed, of course, that he has timed his tour so that he would

arrive in New Orleans in time for the Mardi Gras. I suppose I should not be too critical of Joab—he can't help his nature, and his ballyhoo visits *do* help the popular morale. I would even be enthusiastic about them, if only he could render us some real assistance. But I'm afraid his capabilities do not go beyond speech-making."

Jimmy's eyes were watching the Triumvir's face, trying to determine what was behind that worry-furrowed brow. Andrew Warren was a loyal man. He would not have admitted suspicion of one of his associates, even if he entertained it. But Jimmy wondered whether Warren really believed that Joab Burley, with his handshaking and continual political powwows, was really as innocuous as he seemed....

"The other reason for my being here is Hugh Delcourt, out in Santa Fe," Jimmy switched the subject and produced the telegram and radiogram that had preceded David Delcourt's death.

Briefly, he recounted what had happened in New York—

while Andrew Warren's eyes became more haggard and his shoulders drooped as if a weight were being fastened on them.

"Mexicans," he said slowly. "That means there can be little doubt that Ferrara is right."

"I have been trying to reach Hugh Delcourt by wire, but there is no response," Jimmy added. "Silence seems to have blanketed Santa Fe, which means that there is something on foot down there—something of vital importance. Delcourt must be in constant danger—that is the only reason for his extreme precautions and for his silence. Whatever he has discovered seems to be linked up with developments south of the Rio Grande—and that means my place is down there beside him to find out just what is afoot."

Andrew Warren looked steadily, with undisguised affection, at the tall, poised, confident young man who rose and stood facing him. Jimmy Christopher's well knit, athletic body was eloquent of smooth, rippling strength. His clear eyes, his well shaped features beneath a thatch of sandy hair, bespoke clean living and an intelligence that was ready to grapple with any problem at a moment's notice. He was a man in a million, and yet he might have passed as any one of his fellow citizens— might have gone unnoticed in a crowd. Certainly his youthful appearance gave no indication of the deeds he performed, of the tremendous responsibilities that had rested upon him.

The Savior of America, they called Operator 5—and yet this man who had, almost single-handed, preserved a nation and dragged it back from the brink of destruction, was little more than an overgrown boy....

Andrew Warren's eyes misted, as he clasped the outstretched hand and gripped the square, lithe-muscled shoulder.

"Go ahead, Jimmy—and may God bless you," he said softly. "You are a clever man, I know that—but one of the most farsighted things you ever did was when you refused to let them elect you to the Triumvirate. I think—" he glanced around the walls of his office resignedly—"you would have died if they had penned you up in a cell like this."

And as he left, Jimmy Christopher knew just how much that mild-mannered, sturdy old New Englander, who stayed steadfast in his place at the helm of the nation, wished that he could unchain himself from his desk and share the perils which lay waiting in the far Southwest….

JIMMY WAS hardly out of the building, striding down Pennsylvania Avenue, when he was overtaken by a trim, blue-uniformed figure and turned to recognize Colonel MacBride, chief of the Washington police.

"No, I don't have a warrant for you, Operator 5." MacBride grinned an answer to his jocular greeting. "But the New York City police are very much interested in one of your companions. They have had me on the phone and asked me to pick up a Doctor Norman King and hold him until detectives can reach here with a murder warrant. When I learned that King came to Washington with you, I held off action until I had a chance to see you."

"That murder charge has all the earmarks of a stall or a frame-up, Colonel," Jimmy decided quickly. "King was with me all the while he was in New York—and he almost became a corpse rather than a killer. Come up to the hotel and perhaps we can get to the bottom of this. I have an engagement with King there at six."

But the moment Jimmy opened the door of his suite, and stepped into the foyer, he stopped in amazement. The place was turned upside-down, his papers and belongings had been thoroughly ransacked and tossed aside when they proved disappointing—and in the middle of the disordered room lay the body of Dalbert Eastman with a bullet through the center of his forehead!

Jimmy knelt beside the body, lifted the dead man's hand and found that the fingers were already chilled. Then he was on his toes, going over every inch of that room in search of possible clues. When he was finished, he had found just one significant item—and that was Dr. Norman King's slouch hat, which lay trampled on the floor!

Quickly, Jimmy stepped to the phone and asked to be connected with Dr. King's room. There was no answer—and he started post-haste to the office for a passkey. With Colonel MacBride at his side, he opened the door and stepped in to investigate. This time, no tragedy confronted them. King's bags were there as he had left them, his suits hung in the closet—but he was gone. Gone so thoroughly that the alarm MacBride sent out for him failed to locate him anywhere in the city.

Back in his own suite, Jimmy watched Dalbert Eastman's body being removed to the morgue. The pier guard's warning words flashed back into his mind. Eastman had been suspicious of King from the moment he learned that the doctor had arrived on the *Tremont*.

"We don't know anything about this man," he had fretted. "He says he attended young Delcourt when he was stabbed on the boat—but we have no way of knowing that it wasn't King who tried to murder Delcourt. He was too ready there on the spot the minute Delcourt was shot down—too anxious to stick close to you. I don't trust him."

And now Dalbert Eastman was dead….

The murder of young Delcourt, the ambush attack on himself in New York, the murder warrant for King, the ransacking of this suite and murder of Eastman—all, Jimmy Christopher was convinced, were designed to keep him away from Santa Fe, to delay him as much as possible if he could not be stopped entirely. For some reason, it was supremely important to somebody that he be kept out of the Southwest—and for that reason he was going there immediately, without waiting until morning as he had intended.

A few minutes on the telephone, and he had chartered a special air-liner to speed him to the New Mexico capital—and had arranged to take a companion who had shared many of his most hazardous exploits.

"Will I be ready by eight o'clock?" young Tim Donovan whooped. "All I have to do is grab my hat and I'm ready now!"

TIM WAS there at the new Hoover Flying Field, waiting, when Jimmy Christopher arrived—and a single glance at the expression which wreathed his freckled, pug-nosed face left no doubt of the bond of affection which existed between these two.

Ever since the night, years before, when Tim, hungry and shivering in a dark New York hallway, had saved Jimmy Christopher from a criminal's bullet and had been taken into the undercover ace's life, there had been nothing in his world to compare with the admiration and devotion he lavished on his idol.

Those feelings were not one-sided. It had taken Jimmy but a short while to discover that he had found a most unusual character in the ragged little bootblack. In that small, wiry body flamed a spirit that was undaunted. Since that time, Tim Donovan, hardly out of his teens, had seen more of adventure and deadly peril than is the lot of most men during a long lifetime. And in those years of constant hazard and danger he had proved himself as a tried and trusted assistant who could be depended upon in any crisis.

For hours they sat in the cabin of the plane, speculating on what lay ahead of them, while the liner sped through the night and bore them steadily toward the answers to their questions. It was nearly midnight before they were ready to retire. Jimmy was going forward to have a word with the pilots before turning in, and Tim started back to the washroom. But—the moment he opened the door of the little cubicle, he stood petrified—then came dashing back into the cabin wide-eyed.

"There's a dead man in there!" he gasped. "A corpse—he toppled out when I opened the door!"

Jimmy Christopher was already past him, yanking the door wide—to stare down at the blood-soaked heap that was Dr. Norman King!

The man seemed to have been knifed in dozens of places. His

clothes were cut to ribbons and dyed red with his blood—but, amazingly, there still was a spark of life in him. By some miracle, those lethal thrusts had reached no vital spot, and the gaping wounds had matted shut before he had lost sufficient blood to bleed to death.

Now that King's position had been disturbed, some of the ghastly wounds had ripped open again, and fresh blood was crimsoning the floor.

Quickly, Jimmy lifted the limp body and bore it out into the cabin aisle to stretch it on the floor. Stripping off the tattered coat and shirt, he stopped the bleeding as best he could, while Tim brought water and trickled some between the slack lips. Gradually, King came back to semi-consciousness. For a moment, his glassy eyes flickered open and stared around him uncomprehendingly. His lips moved, but not even a whisper of sound came from them.

Certainly the man needed medical attention at once, but the surest way to get him to a hospital was to continue right on to Santa Fe, Jimmy considered quickly. To attempt a landing in the dark might only mean disaster—and even if the pilot found a landing field he could negotiate there might be no hospital within miles of it.

"There is an emergency kit on board, Tim," he made his decision. "Get it from the pilots. With that, we'll have to do the best we can."

The kit provided pads and bandages, disinfectant to wash the wounds before they were taped up, and a sedative to send the suffering physician back into complete unconsciousness. Neither

Jimmy nor Tim Donovan left his side during the remainder of that flight. A dozen times during the night Jimmy felt for the heart that had so miraculously escaped the murderous blades, and each time the beat was faintly discernible.

Norman King clung doggedly to life—and as Jimmy Christopher looked down at the still, pallid face he wondered what could be the meaning of this latest outrage. Why had King been stabbed so viciously and left for dead? And why had his body been propped up there in the washroom of the special plane where Operator 5 would be sure to find it?

A grim warning of what awaited him in Santa Fe? That appeared to be the answer—and now the speeding plane seemed to be leaden-weighted; seemed to crawl through the night at a snail's pace....

CHAPTER 3
WAR CLOUDS

T HE LIGHTS of Santa Fe were twinkling out as the air-liner hovered above the city and glided into the airport. It was another twenty minutes before Jimmy Christopher could get a taxicab, and full dawn before the wounded man was carried into the hospital.

"This man hasn't any right to be living today." The physician in charge shook his head, after he had examined the patient. "But since you have managed to keep him alive this long, we may be able to pull him through."

"How soon do you think he will be able to talk, Doctor?" Jimmy wanted to know, but the medico's face was discouraging.

"Can't say," he shrugged. "Maybe tomorrow, but I doubt it. It will be best for him if he stays in a coma a few days while he rallies his strength—otherwise I doubt that he will know what he is saying anyway."

So any hope of immediate information from the lips of Norman King was ended, Jimmy realized, as he and Tim left the sick room. It was still too early to call at the modest home that served Hugh Delcourt as an executive mansion, but the city was beginning to stir into wakefulness. They would have time to walk across town; might have an opportunity to get some idea of what was responsible for Delcourt's alarm.

The first inkling of the uneasiness that was gnawing at the nerves of Santa Fe came as they reached the office of the *Courier*. Even at that early hour a number of citizens were gathered in front of the plate-glass windows, looking up at the bulletins pasted on them.

"Three thousand more Japanese landed at Mazatlan in the past week!" one of those bulletins read; and beside it was another: "Sonora and Sinaloa now almost entirely in Japanese hands, according to returned traveler who barely escaped jail for his investigation."

"Don't see how they come to let him get through," a craggy-featured old gray-beard commented to Jimmy. "They keep everything covered so slick that nobody gets a notion of what goes on—an' when anybody does, he just disappears, that's all."

"Yuh don't have to see to know what's goin' on down there,"

another chimed in bitterly. "They're movin' an army in right under our noses—and soon as they're ready they're comin' north. And who's gonna stop them—tell me that? Ferrara and a handful of men diggin' ditches in the sand?"

"Ferrara's only down here to pull the wool over our eyes and keep us quiet," a burly rancher endorsed. "The Canadian border is all that counts with Andy Warren—the hell with us down here; we can shift for ourselves. Don't expect any help from Washington, friend. If there's anything going to be done for us, we gotta do it ourselves."

It took but a few moments of that sort of talk to swell the group to a score—and every one who spoke, Jimmy noted, was pessimistic and bitter. These people were afraid. They felt that they were in the path of an invasion that might sweep down upon them at any moment—felt that they had been neglected and abandoned by the rest of the nation.

Their fear was understandable, but this hostility to Andrew Warren and the national government was amazing. As he listened, Jimmy Christopher became convinced that it had been deliberately incited. Someone was at work down there in the Southwest sowing the seeds of discontent that, fanned by fear, might blossom into open rebellion!

That must be what was alarming Hugh Delcourt. Perhaps

he had discovered the identity of the troublemakers and was in danger from them.

Jimmy waited to hear no more. Quickly he led the way to the Delcourt home and rang the bell. But the old Indian doorman shook his head and said that the governor wasn't home. Nobody knew where he was or when he would be back.

"But there must be some way I can get in touch with him," Jimmy insisted. "There must be someone who knows where he is. I am from Washington, from his son David—"

"Never mind, I'll attend to it, Atzo," a soft voice spoke at the old man's shoulder, and Delcourt's pretty young daughter was in the doorway. "You—you must be from Operator 5?" Her guarded question found an answer in Jimmy's eyes, and she stepped back to invite them inside. "Oh, I am so glad you came," escaped from her impetuously the moment they were seated in the living-room. "Father has disappeared, and there hasn't been a word from David...."

Her dark eyes were keen, searching; they must have read the message Tim Donovan tried to conceal by averting his face.

"You said you were from David," she reminded Jimmy. "Yet you couldn't be here so quickly unless—unless something has happened to him! Something *has*—I can see it in your eyes! Operator 5 sent you here to tell us about it!"

"I am Operator 5, Miss Delcourt," Jimmy told her quietly, and then, as gently as possible, he told her how her brother had added his name to the roll of his country's immortals.

"He was murdered!" the girl half-sobbed. "Now I *know* that something has happened to Father. He disappeared three days ago without a word to anybody—just left the house for his office and didn't come back. We have not announced his disappearance because we know that he has been greatly worried about the situation in Mexico. Sam Blankenship—he is Father's right-hand man; his adjutant, I believe he calls him—thinks that he may be doing some investigation that would be endangered if we gave the story to the newspapers. Sam thinks that he will come back safely, but I am afraid, Operator 5. It isn't like Father to slip away that way without telling me—he is always so considerate. But lately he has been acting very peculiarly. He hasn't seemed to be himself—"

"Peculiar in what way, Miss Delcourt?" Jimmy prompted.

"He has been so secretive." For a moment she stopped, tried to find words to express her thoughts. "It has almost seemed as if he was afraid—afraid of everyone around him… if you can imagine that of Hugh Delcourt."

If Hugh Delcourt was afraid, it was not for himself, Jimmy Christopher knew. There was not a drop of cowardly blood in the old fighter's body; not a thought of personal danger in his mind. And yet his keen-eyed daughter was not likely to have been deceived….

There was not much more information that she could furnish. After a few more minutes of conversation Jimmy excused himself and led the way to the governor's office—and Sam Blankenship.

IN THE days before the Purple Wars, Blankenship had made a name for himself as an adventurer and soldier-of-fortune from one end of Central America to the other. Whenever a new revolution had broken out in one of the Latin republics, Sam Blankenship was quite certain to be found leading or directing it—if he had not been hired to take charge of the government forces and suppress it. Like a stormy petrel, he had bounced from one opéra bouffe war to another, until real war had engulfed all of America—and then he had served his country with distinction.

Now, a broad-shouldered giant of a man in his early forties, he sat at a desk in the office next to the governor's and rose with a wide smile of recognition when Jimmy Christopher and Tim Donovan were announced.

"No need to ask you why you are here, Operator 5," he greeted. "You want to know where to find Hugh Delcourt—and I wish to God I could tell you. I have been telling Hazel that he must be doing some undercover work and that he'd be back safe and sound. At first, I believed that… but now I don't know."

His strong hand cupped his chin and his fingers massaged his leathery cheeks as his sun-wrinkled eyes half-closed.

"Things are pretty bad down here, you know." He peered at Jimmy half-questioningly. "No matter what the rest of the country thinks, we are convinced that an invasion from Mexico is inevitable—and we are doing what we can to prepare for it. Delcourt and I have been working in close contact. We've been organizing informal militia units all through the state and the surrounding territory—men who are drilling and getting ready to defend their homes when the storm breaks."

He nodded. "We've been trying to keep that as quiet as possible, but there are eyes watching and ears listening all around us. Delcourt has been doing his best to find direct evidence of an

JIMMY CHRISTOPHER

invasion plot—and that may be the reason he left his home for the office and never arrived here."

Hugh Delcourt had been on the right track. He had been

within grasp of the evidence he was seeking—Jimmy Christopher was certain of that by the end of the day. His investigation had uncovered nothing that gave any indication of the governor's fate, but he was convinced that Delcourt's disappearance had not been voluntary.

Those thoughts were still coursing through his worried brain after he had retired and lay sleepless in his bed. Again and again, he went over what he had learned—then suddenly he froze, every muscle tense, as his eyes stared fixedly at the window. Slowly, barely creeping, his right hand stole toward the holstered automatic on the chair beside him. He watched a black shape rise in the patch of lighter darkness, and saw it take the form of a man.

Jimmy's finger tightened on the trigger, and the gun muzzle was trained on the center of that dark bulk. But, instead of trying to enter, the intruder tapped gently on the windowpane. For an instant, a tiny flashlight played on a high-cheek-boned face and then snapped out.

"It is I—Richard Wilson," a deep voice spoke softly from the darkness. "I have news of the governor, Operator 5—may I enter?"

Richard Wilson—that was the young college-bred Indian who was Hugh Delcourt's secretary. Jimmy had met him briefly during the day, thought the fellow taciturn, almost surly.

"Okay, enter," he granted permission. "But remember—there is an automatic trained on your belly every second."

Noiselessly, the Indian stepped through the window and drew the shade after him. Not until he had darkened both windows did he flash on his light and stand it on end so that its reflected glow feebly lit up the room.

"I can understand your caution," he nodded. "I, too, was cautious until I was certain of you. But now, if you will dress quickly and come with me, I can take you to one who will give you the information you seek. No—" he held up his hand— "there is no time to talk. You probably are watched here, and may have been followed. We have to leave without delay."

And that was all the information Jimmy could get from him, as he followed the Indian out through the window, along a balcony and down to the rear of the hotel, where two saddled horses stood waiting. Silently, they rode out of town, and, once clear of the buildings, the drum of their horses' hooves was the only sound.

"We are there," Richard Wilson announced at last, and in another moment the shadowy outlines of flat-topped adobe structures began to arise in front of them—the buildings of an Indian pueblo.

IN FRONT of the largest structure in the settlement Wilson dismounted and led the way through a low doorway—into a dimly lighted room where a wan skeleton of a man lay on a rug-covered bed. For a moment, Jimmy Christopher stared at that emaciated face incredulously. Then he strode forward to bend over the bed and grasp the bony hand of Emmet O'Connor, one of his best men, who was supposed to be in Mazatlan, on the west coast of Mexico!

O'Connor was barely alive, but he managed to open his eyes,

managed a faint smile of greeting that barely moved the muscles of his face.

"I'm finished, Operator 5," he whispered, "but I'm glad you got here—before I go. I almost got through safely—got within five miles of the border—before they rode me down and shot me to pieces. They left me there for dead. But I managed to hang on—and then crawl the rest of the way—over the line. One of Ferrara's men found me and took me to Delcourt—and afterward he brought me here."

He stirred. "Those Jap farmers are a blind, Operator 5. They are trained soldiers. Their 'wives' are men—soldiers in disguise. Their 'farm machinery' is tanks and armored trucks and guns. There are close to a hundred and fifty thousand of them waiting for the signal to sweep up over the border. Their General Isogai is in Mexico City working with the Mexicans—laying out the plans…."

Crimson froth bubbled from his lips, and a tremor shook him. Anxiously, the Indian medicine-man bent over him and mumbled, "No should talk." But Emmet O'Connor forced his eyes to open, forced his stiffening lips to frame the words that were burning in his brain.

"Toledaro—he's only a puppet," he gasped. "He is completely—under the domination—of a personal emissary—from the Jap emperor. I couldn't learn—his identity. But he's the big boss—in Mexico City. He has them all fooled—tricked—"

The last word faded off into nothing, but there was a smile of triumph on Emmet O'Connor's skeletal face as the death rattle clogged his throat. His ordeal was over, that ghastly trip

34

from five miles across the border finished at last when he had reported to his chief!

So this was the news that Hugh Delcourt had tried so hard to convey to Operator 5. This was the news for which David Delcourt had died and his father had disappeared….

As Jimmy Christopher looked down pityingly at that wasted body on the bed, he realized that his worst fears were substantiated. The Japanese invaders he had feared were an actuality—and against a mechanized force of a hundred and fifty thousand trained Japanese soldiers, the makeshift defenses which Ferrara was throwing up along the border would be utterly useless. Once that invasion got underway, the entire Western half of the United States was doomed.

It must be stopped—but how? There was only one possible way.

"Those invaders must be prevented from crossing the border. The 'preventing' must be done in Mexico, must be accomplished at any cost—"

So engrossed was he with his problem that he completely forgot his surroundings. He did not realize he had spoken aloud—until another voice sounded.

"Exactly," Richard Wilson said gravely, "and that is where I and my people will be able to help. Remember that we Apaches are also Americans—and in this perhaps we can serve our country even better than our white brothers!"

CHAPTER 4
SECOND A.E.F.

A T FIRST there seemed to be nothing more than a puff of dust blowing across the arid New Mexico plain from the direction of thirty-mile-distant Santa Fe—but gradually the dust cloud took shape and became the figures of two sweaty, grimy-faced horsemen riding side by side. Once there had been an excellent road leading from the main concrete highway to the Three Star ranch—but that was before the hordes of the Purple Empire had swept over the country like a plague of locusts. Now it was simpler to pick a trail between the scattered clumps of sagebrush and bunch grass.

Silently the riders jogged along, but their keen eyes were constantly probing into the distance. For miles they had seemed to be the only two humans in all that semi-wasteland. But as they approached the pass between two low-lying hills, that was the Three Star's natural gateway, another dust cloud came toward them. Gradually it resolved itself into a tall, lanky, dejected-looking rider who was even more dust-covered than they.

"Hiyah," he greeted as he reined up his mount a few yards from them. "Hotter'n the hinges o' hell—an' I got thirty more miles o' this ahead o' me."

"Hot," one of the pair nodded; then, "Where you from—the Three Star?"

"Thought I was goin' to be," the lanky one spat disgustedly, "but it seems they didn't appreciate my exceptional qualifications."

"They're hirin', ain't they?" the spokesman for the duo asked. "We heard up in Santa Fe they was takin' on hands."

"So'd I—" the solitary rider shrugged—"but that's another o' these here desert whispers. Nothin' to it. The couple hands they got are sittin' around dodgin' the sun. You're wastin' your time goin' on now."

The duo eyed each other questioningly, uncertainly; but again the spokesman made their decision. "Come this far—guess we'll ride on and have a look at the layout. Horses need waterin' anyway."

Then they were moving on, stirring the dust into another cloud that rolled toward the narrow pass. The lone rider also resumed his way. But his eyes turned backward and watched the pair until they had disappeared—and by then, he knew, other sharp eyes from vantage points on the hillsides were following their every movement.

The Three Star proved to be all that he had described it. There was no sign of cattle around the place, and the dilapidated buildings had an air of desertion. A frowsy-looking ranch-hand answered their halloo and regarded them with slight favor.

"Jobs?" he grunted. "Hell, there ain't no jobs here—none 'cept the ones me an' Tobe an' Hilo Pete has, an' we're not lookin' for competition. Been a reg'lar procession out here the past two-three days. Must be some loco idjit's idea of a joke."

The riders watered their horses and looked over the place with shrewd eyes that missed nothing. Again they eyed each other.

"That's what comes o' listenin' to every barroom rumor." The spokesman shrugged resignedly, and he led the way back into the trail—to be followed by watchful spy-glasses until their dust cloud blotted out entirely.

HALF A dozen times that day riders, singly and in groups, came over that trail; and each time the tall, dejected looking horseman rode out to meet them. But instead of trying to discourage them he sent them on to the ranch and waved a farewell after them. Sharp-eyed, capable-looking guides greeted them when they dismounted and led them back into the rear of the main building—where Jimmy Christopher sat at a battered table that was serving as a desk.

One by one he interviewed them and passed them on to his assistants to be welded into the organization he was building—a strangely assorted company on which he was staking the fate of the United States!

John Two Eagles, Henry Wide Lake, Charles Morning Sun—dark-skinned, beady-eyed Apaches who came with Richard Wilson's endorsement. Jose Sanchez, Fidel Castro, Domingo Villareal—olive-hued, wide-featured Americans of Mexican descent who had been recommended by trusted agents in all parts of the Southwest.

"Juan Perez," Jimmy glanced through the cabalistic note a small, swarthy-skinned applicant had presented. "Your great-grandfather fought under Santa Ana at the Alamo?"

"*Si*, señor," the dark eyes twinkled, "but he was my *great-grand-father*—and since his day the Perez family have been citizens of New Mexico. There were many of us, but now I, alone, remain—Emperor Rudolph's men accounted for the rest. So I, alone, can make reparation for my ancestor's mistake. All that I ask is an opportunity to serve in any capacity against the tyrant Toledaro."

Peter Calhoun, Edward Weaver, Mark Crosby—they had served for years in the Texas and Arizona Rangers. Asher Stewart, Floyd Hood, James Conklin and Dell Thompson—they had been peace officers and border patrolmen before the Purple regime drove them into hiding.

Added to those hand-picked recruits, who knew the Southwest and Mexico like the palms of their hands, were Andy Bretton, Jim Spencer, Ira Hardy and a dozen other survivors of the Suicide Battalion that had gone to Europe with Operator 5 less than a year ago; veterans of that stalwart legion whose sacrifices had given America a new lease on life.

One by one, Operator 5 interviewed those level-eyed, stern-jawed volunteers who plodded along the dusty trail to the Three Star. One by one, he shook them by the hand and added their names to the roster of the unknowns, the silent workers whose existence their fellow citizens would never even suspect.

Stalwart young men, solid middle-aged ones, and canny-eyed oldsters—age did not matter in that recruiting, except in a few rare instances. That was what old Ben Nolan tried to argue, but Jimmy Christopher shook his head regretfully as he refused the frail old-timer.

"You've done your share time and again, Ben," he tried to assuage the old man's disappointment. "This is a job for younger men. I'll keep you in mind, and if there is anything you can do here—"

"Too old!" Nolan scoffed, and his faded blue eyes snapped

angrily. "I can outlast any o' these infants you're taking on. I was doing undercover work before you were born, Jimmy. I served with your daddy, Q-6—he wouldn't think I'm too old."

"But he isn't coming with us either, Ben," Jimmy reminded. "I know how you feel, but wait. There may be something that will come up here—something that only you can handle."

The slim, stooped old desert-prowler was still snorting as he headed back to Santa Fe, and Jimmy watched him go with genuine regret. It was hard to turn down a man like Ben Nolan, but to take him into Mexico would be tantamount to sending him straight to his death….

"Our mission this time will be no less perilous—even more dangerous than it was in Europe," Jimmy Christopher told his men. "There is little chance to cause dissension between the Mexicans and the Japanese. Toledaro is too anti-American and hand-in-glove with the Japs to be influenced by anything of that sort—and his grip on the country is too mail-fisted to give us any hope that his advisors might be influenced to overrule him. Our only hope is to awaken the Mexican people to their own danger—to arouse them against Toledaro and take the lead in overthrowing him."

He went on. "The moment he learns what is afoot, he will try to stamp out mercilessly the least sign of discontent. An adobe wall and a firing squad will be your reward, if you are captured preaching sedition—and yet those of you who handle that part of our campaign will have a better chance of survival than those who help me to carry on the guerrilla sabotage that will cripple the invaders and blunt their effectiveness."

He told them. "This is a second A.E.F. we are enlisting—but it will go into action with no flags and music, with no stirring farewells. It does not even offer you a reverently tended hero's grave. We are going into oblivion once we put foot on Mexican soil—but that is our only hope of saving America from bloody conquest and slavery."

They said very little, but their expressions spoke volumes. Narrow-eyed and tight-lipped, they listened to him—and he had his answer in the firm, determined clasp of their hands.

IN THE week following Emmet O'Connor's death Operator 5 had lost no time in make his plans for the penetration of Mexico. Establishing his headquarters at the Three Star, he had sent out his call for volunteers by the trusted "grapevine" that was more effective than any broadcasting system. Quickly he had gathered around him a staff of trained assistants who took the recruits in hand and gave them as thorough a grounding in the tricks of espionage as was possible in such a limited time.

As soon as they were ready they came to him for their orders, and one by one they shook his hand and went their way. Standing in the ranch house doorway, he watched two young stalwarts riding off into the distance—and his thoughts flashed back to that other company of heroes who had clasped his hand and stepped onto the ships that, in most cases, bore them into the waiting arms of Death.

How many of these, he wondered, would come back? How many would he ever see again? How many would be left, bullet-riddled corpses, beneath the hot Mexican sun until the vultures had disposed of them?

Subconsciously his eyes glanced up into the sky, where an airplane was winging its way in the direction of Santa Fe.

"It is the same plane," Richard Wilson commented as he lowered the field-glasses through which he had been studying the machine. "It has been passing back and forth over this ranch every day for nearly a week—and there is nothing in this wilderness to interest it. Nothing but us...."

Jimmy had noticed the frequency of that plane's appearances, but at that moment he was less concerned with the maneuvers of the aerial visitor than with his failure to hear from Tim Donovan, whom he had left behind in Santa Fe. Tim was to have kept an eye on developments in the city and to have reported anything significant that developed—but it was now three days since there had been word of any sort from him.

And in the morning Jimmy would have to leave, without an opportunity to return to the town....

FOR TWO days after Jimmy Christopher left Santa Fe, Tim Donovan explored the city from end to end and talked with everyone who could be led into a conversation. That was not difficult, for the town was seething with excitement. But it was not what was said so much as what was left unsaid, the conversations which stopped abruptly when the speaker suddenly realized that he had started to say too much—that convinced Tim that there was something of supreme importance on foot. On the second night he had migrated as usual to the front of the *Courier* office and was scanning the latest bulletin.

" 'Border wide open to invasion,' says Colonel Philips," it

announced. "Former state adjutant sees entire West helpless if Japanese strike."

A crowd of nearly a hundred men and women were indignantly discussing the situation, but there was nothing new in their remarks—until a young fellow, whose breath reeked with the spicy odor of fiery tequila, grinned at Tim and jerked his head contemptuously at the others.

"That's what *they* think," his grin broadened. "We're just helpless—just settin' here and waitin' for the Japs to come and mow us down. Sure, that's all—just a helpless bunch o' babies. But maybe they don't know as much as they think they do, see?"

"Maybe you're right," Tim quickly led him on. "But I don't see what chance Ferrara would have—"

"Who said anything about Ferrara?" his new acquaintance demanded. "Ferrara—we don't need him. We can take care of ourselves!" His voice lowered to a throaty whisper. "Never heard of Sam Blankenship's defense battalions, did you? *Defense* battalions—yeah, that's good!" and his right eye closed in a heavy-lidded wink.

"Yes, I've heard something about a defense battalion," Tim admitted gravely. "I've been trying to locate someone who knows something about the outfit and can take me there. If there's going to be trouble, I want to do my part."

"Well, you've come to the right *hombre.*" His companion wagged his head enthusiastically. "Lee Pearson—that's my name. And I sure can set you right. Tomorrow night—that's the drill night—you can meet me and go along."

Tim Donovan quickly completed the arrangements for

their meeting and was on hand the next evening when Pearson arrived. The young fellow, now much more cautious than on the night before, led the way across town to what had been built to serve as a food warehouse in the starvation months following the liberation from the yoke of the Purple Empire. Now the big, barn-like structure was being used as a drilling place for a company of nearly two hundred young men who were earnestly engaged in bayonet practice, when Tim and his sponsor finally arrived.

After being introduced to the commanding officer, Tim watched the drill for half an hour and then asked to be enrolled in the company. Given a rifle, he was mustered into a squad and spent the next hour marching and charging from one end of the improvised armory to the other. During that time, his vigilance never ceased. His companions, he noticed, evinced a natural interest in the newcomer. But, as the drill progressed, he felt more and more that he was being studied; that curious eyes were watching and probing him. Half a dozen times he caught a glimpse of queer, enigmatical expressions in eyes that turned away the moment he noticed them. Before he was ready to rack his gun, at the conclusion of the drill, he was certain that there was something more to this organization than appeared on the surface.

When the battalion was dismissed, he left the armory with the others, but a block from it he doubled back to the building in a roundabout direction. For some time the battalion members continued to come out in ones and twos, but at last they all seemed to have left.

Cautiously Tim approached the door and slipped inside. The large main room that had been used for the drill was dark, but he caught the low rumble of voices. That was coming from one side, where there were several smaller rooms used as headquarters by the officers.

Silently he picked his way down the corridor, until he reached a door from beneath which a strip of light showed—a thin wooden door through which he could easily make out what was being said inside. For a moment he could not catch the drift of the conversation—and then found it was himself who was being discussed!

"That new chap, Donovan—how about him?" someone asked.

"Pearson brought him in—but didn't okay him," another voice gruffed testily. "We can't take chances on anyone who comes along—you oughta know that, Rayburn."

"I was watching him," the first speaker answered. "He knows how to handle a gun and might make good material."

"Handling a gun is the least important," a gruff voice rasped. "We need men we know are okay—men who know how to keep their mouths shut and who haven't a lot of fool ideas about listening to Andy Warren."

This *was* the hotbed of discontent that Operator 5 had been trying to ferret out! As Tim listened, his amazement and indignation increased. This organization he had joined only pretended to be a defense outfit, he soon discovered. The defense battalion was being used merely as a blind to cover up a smaller, more select group that was being armed to the teeth and whipped into shape as a crack military unit to take the *offensive* at a moment's notice! A unit that planned not to wait for the Japanese to come across the border, but to invade Mexico!

With infinite caution, he fingered the knob and opened the door on a thin slit so that he could see into the room. There were some thirty men gathered there—and among them he recognized those who had been eyeing him so curiously. Thirty men whose mad scheme might prove to be the spark that would start a war that would mean the end of America!

For long moments he stared at those faces, tried to ingrain them on his memory so that he would be able to identify them for Jimmy Christopher—for Jimmy must know of this immediately. Noiselessly he closed the door and released the knob—only to be seized and borne to the floor by strong arms that wrapped around him from behind!

Desperately Tim fought, but they were too many for him. They overwhelmed him, pinned him down so that he could not move a limb—and then the door was flung open and the corridor was flooded with light. Into the room they dragged him—and he discovered that his captors were Lee Pearson and several of his battalion mates.

"Pretty clever, ain't you?" Pearson grinned at him as they tied his wrists and ankles. "Only this time you weren't as smart as you thought you were. You tumbled beautifully for my drunk act last night—came right along like a baby and stuck your neck in the noose we had waiting for you. Too bad, Donovan—it looks like Operator 5 will have to do without his clever young assistant for a while. Till we get back from Mexico, anyway!"

Helplessly Tim was carried outside and thrust into the back of a car that soon left the lights of Santa Fe behind and drove off into the blackness of the night.

CHAPTER 5
DREAMS OF EMPIRE

"WELCOME JOAB BURLEY!" the hundred-foot banner stretched across the inside of the Mobile railroad station proclaimed. "Yeh, Burley!" a thousand voices yelled, while a brass band did its best to drown out their clamor. But Diane Elliot yawned as she climbed down from the press car and followed the Triumvir through the cheering crowd.

Savannah, Atlanta, Birmingham, Montgomery and at dozens of way-stations in between—everywhere it had been the same. For days she had been listening to a lot of empty, windy speeches, and sending monotonous accounts of them back to her papers. "The best radio-speaking voice since William Jennings Bryan's," the critics had hailed Joab Burley's warm and penetratingly resonant tones—but Diane was thoroughly tired of hearing them blare forth from amplifiers.

During the past two weeks she had seen sufficient of the peregrinating Triumvir to shatter any illusions of him she might have had. Joab Burley was a politician, and he would never be anything more than that. Like most of his type, he was thoroughly at home in those two strangely opposite settings—basking in the limelight in front of a crowd and hidden away in secret conferences with gentlemen of questionable repute.

Those conferences were never mentioned in the newspaper accounts, but Diane had been giving them more and more of her attention—and as she did her suspicions of Joab Burley increased. There was an uneasiness, almost a furtiveness, about the man when he was out of the public eye that was unmistakable; and she had noticed that it had been increasing greatly in the past few days. Unless she missed her bet by a wide margin, Burley was heading into something that had him worried as well as excited....

That night in Mobile those thoughts were very much in her mind, as she finished her account of his almost stereotyped speech and gave it to a telegraph operator. Burley seemed more anxious than usual to get away from the crowd that evening, and several times she had noticed him glancing nervously at his watch. Curiously she trailed him as he left the hall, followed his car in a cab. But he was driven straight to his hotel and apparently retired.

"Wrong again," she told herself as she went to her own room.

But something of Burley's uneasiness seemed to have communicated itself to her. After she got into bed, she tossed restlessly and could not fall asleep. Finally she gave up the attempt and again put on her clothes to go out to a drugstore for something to drink.

Impatiently she ticked the elevator button—and then decided not to wait for the car but to walk down the two flights to the street. The stairway at the end of the hall led down to a side entrance, and just as she stepped out onto the street she caught a glimpse of Joab Burley getting into a car that stood with running motor at the curb.

The machine was underway, speeding down the street, before she could locate a cab to follow it. But she had memorized the number and knew that she would recognize that car again anywhere she saw it. The street down which it had sped led toward the docks—a dark, unfrequented part of town at that time of night, but one in which an automobile would be very conspicuous.

Diane took the little automatic from her handbag and slipped it into the pocket of her suit. With the reassuring feel of its steel grip against her palm, she started toward the bay. In five minutes she had reached the waterfront and was prowling from one dark pier to the next. Negro stevedores were at work on some of the docks, but most of them were dark and silent—long, murky fingers reaching out into the lapping water.

Half an hour she walked and had caught sight of only two cars, one a taxi and the other a light delivery truck. Not a sign of the machine she sought—until she almost stumbled into it! Turned off from the waterfront street, it was parked in the shadow of a pier and might have gone unnoticed had its starter not whirred and its lights flashed on as she approached.

Instantly she drew back into the shadows. A moment later Joab Burley came out of the Stygian tunnel of the covered pier. He was with two men who were talking in a low mumble she could not understand. For a fraction of a second she caught a glimpse of their faces as the car's headlights played full upon them—dark, Spanish-looking faces. Then they were at the car door, obsequiously ushering Burley into it and climbing in after him.

The car sprang into gear almost soundlessly, backed past her, and was out into the street in the space of a few moments. Almost before she realized what had happened, it was gone and she was alone in the darkness. The car was gone—but the pier was still there. And now she might be able to learn what had brought Joab Burley to such a queer rendezvous.

Striving to accustom her eyes to the darkness, she stepped uncertainly toward the pier entrance—and at that moment a hand grasped her arm and an ebon figure loomed in the pool of shadow beside her.

"So the señorita is interested in the Triumvir Burley?" a sibilant voice inquired as steely fingers fastened into her flesh.

But the fellow had made a bad mistake; he had grasped Diane's left arm instead of her right. Instantly her right hand whipped out of the pocket and her automatic clubbed down into his face—again and again as he cursed and staggered back into the pitchy darkness from which he had come.

Before he could clamber back onto his feet, she was running frantically along the street—not stopping until she had reached one of the lighted piers and could sink down on a bollard to catch her breath. Her assailant had made no attempt to follow her, but his voice hissed in her ears even after she was back in the hotel and in bed.

A soft, sibilant voice that had called her señorita; the voice of a Spaniard—or a Mexican. Those two who had climbed into the car after Burley—they were of the same breed. Three Mexicans… now she was almost certain of their nationality.

But why was Joab Burley keeping a midnight rendezvous with two Mexicans on a dark Mobile pier? Surely that was none of his politics—unless it was politics on a scale so huge that it dwarfed her previous opinion of the glad-handing Triumvir.…

DIANE WATCHED him more closely after that. Like a shadow she clung to him when they reached New Orleans. And there again she witnessed his clandestine meetings with several dark-skinned men who were unquestionably Mexicans—men who smiled and fawned upon him as if he were a king.

Until then Diane had been convinced that Jimmy Christopher's half-formed suspicions of the Triumvir were groundless—that the man was nothing more than a preening poseur who liked to hear the sound of his own eloquence. But the sight of those dark-skinned conspirators cast him in a far more dangerous role—a role that Operator 5 ought to hear of at once. And yet Diane had actually witnessed nothing that was incriminating—nothing that might not conceivably have an innocent explanation.…

For hours she debated with herself—and then finally compromised on a telegram to Jimmy that would hold him in readiness to act the moment she had uncovered something definite to report.

Two or three times she worded that telegram and then tore it up before she had the message that satisfied her. She was still thinking about it, as she stepped back from the counter—

and glanced up to catch a pair of dark eyes watching her through the windows. Those eyes narrowed almost imperceptibly and pretended to be reading an advertisement when their owner saw that he had been observed.

Just in time, she remembered those torn blanks with the half-finished messages and went back to retrieve them from the waste basket. Picking them out carefully, she crammed them into her handbag and then left the office—to round the corner and then step back and cross the street to a point from which she could watch through the window.

As she expected, the man with the dark eyes was bending over the basket, sorting through its contents carefully. From there he turned to the counter and started a fruitless argument with the unyielding attendant.

So she was being watched, shadowed.

When she got back to her hotel room, she had added evidence of the interest that was being taken in her. Everything was in its place as she had left it, but she could see that her belongings had been carefully and thoroughly searched while she was away.

From that moment she realized that she must be constantly vigilant—which was especially difficult in New Orleans at that particular season. For the first time since the Purple Invasion, the rebuilt Southern metropolis was holding its historic Mardi Gras carnival. The streets were thronged day and night with gay masqueraders—and with some who might be using their masks for purposes other than merrymaking.

For five days Diane was continually on her guard, but nothing untoward occurred, and by the time the celebration reached its climax with the Coronation Ball on the last night she had almost forgotten her concern in the revelry that surrounded her on every side. Joab Burley was to be an honor guest at the masked ball, and Diane had used the influence of her newspaper syndicate to secure one of the coveted invitations for herself. COSTUMED AS a French shepherdess, she waited in the thronged lobby of her hotel, until a resplendent Jean Lafitte swaggered down the main stairway and out into the crowded street. He was masked like the rest, but she knew his arrogant stride too well to be mistaken in Joab Burley!

Through the dense crowds on St. Charles Street, she followed him until they reached the huge modern hotel that had risen on the ruins of the shell-wrecked St. Charles. Trying to keep track of him in the milling throng that packed the main ballroom was no easy task, but Burley seemed to have no other idea that night than to strut in his finery and dance with as many women as possible.

Before she knew it she was in his arms, listening to the flowery compliments he poured into her ears as he led her around the floor—and hardly had he released her than a handsome young Swiss halberdier claimed her and insisted that the next dance be his.

"I should be jealous of that pirate," he glowered in mock anger. "I've been hunting for you all evening, ever since *you* spurned my offer to escort you here," and Diane recalled that he was one of the young gallants she had laughingly shooed away while she was waiting in the hotel lobby for Joab Burley.

But this time he was not so easily dismissed. When the dance was finished, he mounted guard over her and warned all others away. For nearly half an hour he stayed at her side, pleading and cajoling when she tried to send him away. For a while she entered into the spirit of the play, until suddenly she sensed that he was too persistent—that he was there beside her for a deliberate purpose.

And then she saw that Joab Burley was making his way toward the door—heard him promising to be back shortly!

Now she knew that this doting admirer was no accident. He was there at her side to see that she did not follow the Triumvir!

Diane almost had to tear herself away from him to take refuge in the ladies' room. Right to the door he followed her and then mounted guard outside so that she would not be able to escape. But once she was inside a quick plan flashed into her mind. One of the girls, who was rearranging her mask in front of a mirror, was just about her own size and coloring—a girl in a colonial costume that could be changed quickly.

"Please," Diane begged her, "change with me—for five minutes. It's a man," she giggled; "he's waiting for me outside the door—and I want to fool him. Please put on my costume and go out to him. I will be right after you."

But the girl had already caught the spirit of the lark. Laughingly she traded costumes and walked out to the waiting halberdier… and a moment later Diane slipped through the crowd to the ballroom door, hurried down the stairs to the lobby, and arrived just in time to see Jean Lafitte swaggering out into the carnival-mad street.

Through St. Charles to Canal Street he made his way, and then into the gaily lit Old World streets of the French Quarter. Here the crowd was not so thick and she had little difficulty following him, especially when he turned off into a narrow side street and hurried to historic Jackson Square. Past the dimly lit cathedral he went, and across the Square to the ancient structure that had been a French barracks in the days when New Orleans was part of Napoleon's domain.

Into a dark hallway, halfway down the block, Burley stepped, and when Diane hurried to the door she could hear him clumping up the steps, could hear a door on the second floor opening and closing. A light burned in the windows of the front room on that floor—and a wrought iron grille balcony ran the full length of the block-long building. Two doors farther down there was a sturdy, tree-thick clematis vine that twined around the grille and reached almost to the roof.

That was all Diane needed. Quickly she found a foothold on the gnarled trunk, grasped one of the twisted branches, and climbed the twenty feet to the balcony. Tiptoeing past the dark windows, she crept up to the first one from which light streamed and pressed close to the pane.

Gathered around a central table in the old-fashioned room were six men—Joab Burley and five others who, like himself, were dressed in fantastic costumes and wore black half-length masks over their faces. Even with that partial covering, Diane

Frantically, Diane struggled against the handkerchief—*chloroform!*

could see that three of them had the dark skin and black hair of Mexico's Indian-strain population.

Before them on the table was stretched a large map that absorbed their attention.

"—one column through here," one of the dark-skinned men was saying, as his pencil traced a course across the crackling paper. "Another will be all ready to meet you here. From all sides we close in. Everything is in readiness, señor, everything! We cannot fail. All we need is the word to begin and victory is ours. All of Northern Mexico only awaits the word that you are coming—"

"It will be an empire—a new empire within our grasp!" Joab Burley marveled. His voice was like that of one in a trance as he stared, wide-eyed and rapt, at the fascinating map.

In that moment Diane realized with dismaying certainty that Operator 5's suspicions of this man were all too correct. While Joab Burley had seemed to be wasting time with vainglorious speech-making, he had actually been busily plotting to set himself up as a new emperor in the Southwest! Like Aaron Burr, he had been scheming to establish himself at the head of a new government!

Shocked by that stunning revelation, she crouched there, clutching the window-frame—until suddenly an alarm shrilled in her brain. That hardly audible rasping sound—it came from the balcony; from behind her! Instantly she whirled, but a huge, masked figure towered above her and thick, muscular arms clasped her and held her helpless.

"So our shepherdess has changed her nationality!" a deep

voice rumbled in her ear. "I expected I would find you some-where around here when I discovered how neatly you tricked that numbskull I set to watch you. Well, perhaps this is better."

Frantically Diane struggled, but a handkerchief was pressing down tight over her nose and mouth. Chloroform! The cloying fumes threw her into a frenzied panic, but there was no escaping them. Thick, all-pervading darkness closed in stiflingly upon her—and when she came back to her senses she found that she was lying, tied up securely, on the floor of a cabin plane that was roaring through the night....

CHAPTER 6
GATEWAY TO DEATH

CAREFULLY THE master of the coastwise freighter *Calhoun* steered his course into the mouth of Vera Cruz harbor and stopped the engines while he waited for a pilot. Dubiously he looked at the wizened ancient who came aboard and took the wheel. Slowly the five-thousand-ton vessel got under way and bore steadily to the left, closer and closer to the white concrete walls of the breakwater, while Captain Saunders hovered nervously in the background.

"The channel markings—" he began to protest desperately. But at that moment the *Calhoun* ran her nose solidly into the mud, plowed through it while the pilot held her steadily on her course, and then came to a trembling stop as her propeller churned ineffectually.

With that Saunders blew up. The bridge echoed with his

profane opinion of Mexicans in general and Mexican pilots in particular. But his concern did not even approach that of two passengers who peered out of the windows of one of the cabins. A Mexican of the small shopkeeper class and a Dutch oil operator, they appeared to be—and it was the Dutchman whose stolid, blue-eyed face was the most worried.

"You were right," Jimmy Christopher spoke softly, anxiously. "I only consented to this confounded shift to humor you. I didn't think there was a chance we had been spotted before we left Galveston. But this grounding is no accident—it's too pat."

"Of course," Andy Bretton agreed laconically. "I was certain there had been a leak somewhere. That was why Ben Hatcher was murdered in Galveston; somebody who knew who he was— was waiting for him. Now I know I am right. The reception committee is all arranged. They will come out here all set to grab an innocent-looking Mex shopkeeper and take him to police headquarters for questioning—quite certain that they have their hands on Operator 5. We're walking straight into trouble, and you will be able to handle it lots better out of jail than if they get you behind bars. Don't worry about me; I've come out of tougher spots than this."

But Jimmy Christopher *was* worried. Had he taken Andy Bretton's fears seriously, he never would have consented to the switch of roles Andy had insisted upon after the *Calhoun* left Galveston. If anything, Jimmy had expected that the unwelcome Dutchman might have a more difficult time getting past the hostile eyes of the anti-foreign Mexicans. But now events threatened to take an entirely different course....

Already a small cutter was putting out from shore, and soon it was tied up beside the *Calhoun*—was disgorging a swarm of faded-khaki uniformed Mexican officials who herded the passengers overside to be taken ashore. From his place in the prow of the craft, Jimmy watched the cutter nose up against the breakwater—watched as Andy Bretton, in the stern with several other Mexicans, was promptly surrounded by Mexican police and soldiers, to be marched to a waiting automobile.

The whole thing was handled like clockwork. Without hesitation the police picked out their man and grabbed him before he had a chance even to attempt escape.

"Now it will be my turn," Jimmy expected. Grimly he ran his eyes over the waterfront. He picked out a suave-looking, middle-aged man of uncertain nationality who stood watching from the doorway of one of the customs warehouses—saw him smile and nod with satisfaction as he spoke a few words to the police official who bowed and left his side to take charge of the arresting party.

Immediately the car sped off into town, and, when Jimmy glanced back at the open doorway, the smugly smiling face was no longer there. The watcher had gone—but Jimmy knew that he would recognize the fellow again anywhere that he encountered him.

Once Andy Bretton was gone, the excitement seemed to be over. Phlegmatically the customs officials glanced at the credentials of the rest of the passengers and examined their baggage. Unmolested, they were allowed to go their way; and as Jimmy went to a hotel he knew that Andy Bretton was in grave danger.

THE DAY OF THE DAMNED

The carefully laid trap had closed, and the Mexican secret police were sure that it had delivered Operator 5 into their hands.

IT WAS several hours before Jimmy Christopher left his hotel room, and had the drowsy desk clerk noticed him he would never have recognized the Dutchman to whom he had assigned the sweltering, fly-infested chamber. During those hours Jimmy had dyed his skin and hair, donning the Mexican disguise which he had originally planned to use. Leisurely, he walked toward the center of the town and sauntered into the open front of the Continental Hotel, to sit at one of the tables and order a drink.

He had been there about twenty minutes, watching the collarless, barefooted loungers in the little plaza across the way, when a grimy lottery-ticket salesman approached and begged him to buy. Jimmy dug into his pocket and produced a *peso*.

"*Dies,*" he nodded.

"*Gracias, señor—gracias!*" the vendor thanked him as he counted out ten of the poorly lithographed slips.

With seeming indifference, Jimmy glanced through them as the salesman continued down the street. One was like the other, until he reached the fourth—and eyed a cabalistic jumble of letters that had been penciled on its reverse side.

"Bretton being taken to Mexico City on the five o'clock train," he decoded the message. "Identity still unsuspected."

So far Andy Bretton was safe, but once Andy reached Mexico City death awaited him—if they were satisfied that he was Operator 5. And he would die just as surely if, as was likely, Toledaro's police realized their blunder. Somehow, he must be snatched out of their hands. Perhaps on the train; perhaps in the station in Mexico City….

For some time Jimmy sat there debating his problem. Then he started back to his hotel. He crossed the little plaza, lush with its tropical foliage, and passed the crumbling ruins of the cathedral behind it. A tattered, barefooted beggar, who sat in the shadows of the side doorway arch, whined a plea for alms as he approached. But Jimmy hardly heard him—until suddenly he caught a shifting of those shadows—caught the warning flicker just in time to throw himself forward as the fellow leaped on his back.

Down over Jimmy's left shoulder stabbed an eight-inch blade, so close that it sheared through the cloth of his coat. Then his fingers were gripping the knife-wielder's wrist like a steel trap—holding onto it tenaciously as the fellow's body catapulted headlong and a scream of agony tore from his lips when his arm splintered and wrenched from the shoulder socket.

One scream—and then the man fainted from the pain. Leaving the inert body where it had landed at the foot of the cathedral wall, Jimmie hurried down the street and rounded a corner before anyone had an opportunity to further detain him.

Perhaps that murderous attack was an accident. Perhaps the beggar was a vicious mental case who suddenly went berserk—but more likely he had been deliberately planted there. Also, it was possible an assassin waited in every direction by which Jimmy could have left the Continental. That meant that his disguise had been penetrated—that he must get rid of it at once.

The moment he reached his hotel room, he went to work. Ten

minutes later, the humble middle-class Mexican had become a lordly *hidalgo* who was on his way to the capital for a conference with the *Presidents.*

From a park opposite the railroad station, he waited until Andy Bretton arrived in an automobile well guarded by Mexican soldiers and special agents. Jimmy followed them into the station, bought his ticket and started imperiously toward the train just as the prisoner was being taken aboard. But at that moment wild disturbance broke out at the gateway. Past the ticket inspector rushed the lottery salesman, frantically trying to make his way through the crowd. Desperation blazed in his eyes—and then Jimmy saw why.

Through the crowd raced a savage-faced *peon* clutching a long knife. Straight at the lottery salesman he leaped, and the knife flashed up and down half a dozen times as he held the body of his victim upright and slashed the blood-spurting throat and chest to shreds!

"Ladron!" he screamed as he waved a lottery ticket in the air. "He robbed me! He sold me a ticket for the lottery that is no good!"

Over the mangled body he leaned, still hacking at it frenziedly and shouting vengeful curses, until the police closed in and disarmed him. But when Jimmy Christopher turned to the steps of the railroad car he was sick at heart. That murder had been cold blooded, deliberate—and now faithful Juan Perez had made full reparation for his ancestor's mistake at the Alamo....

Operator 5 had lost another loyal assistant. Instinctively his bleak gaze lifted to the car where Andy Bretton must have seen what had happened and had a foretaste of what might be in store for him—and his eyes clashed again with those of the suave, half-Oriental looking individual he had seen on the customs pier. Again there was a half-smile on that inscrutable face—an inner chuckle of satisfaction that even that bland countenance could not conceal!

CHAPTER 7
DEALER IN DEVIL DRUGS

THE LITTLE apothecary's shop, a block away from the military prison in Mexico City, looked the same as usual the morning after Jimmy Christopher got off the train in the Mexican capital—but it had passed into the hands of a new owner and was about to experience an unprecedented increase in business. Luis Gonzalez, the new proprietor, was a go-getter. He promptly marked down his prices surprisingly, and by that afternoon he had had handbills printed—circulars which were distributed thickly around the soldiers' quarters.

During that day and the next business was brisk. People of all sorts, rich and poor, Mexicans and foreigners, seemed to be attracted by the startling reductions—and many of them seemed to require special treatment or consultations for which they had to go into Gonzalez' back room.

Such a one was the heavily bandaged cripple who limped into the shop on a pair of crutches.

"Well, we did it, Operator 5," he reported. "We just about wiped out the Tehuantepec oil district. There ain't half a dozen wells out there that are still producing. We burned out all the rest, and put a match to the refineries, too. Toledaro won't get much oil from the West Coast for a good long time."

"That's a blow that will handicap them badly, Dell," Jimmy complimented warmly as he patted the old sheriff's shoulder. "A few more successes like that, and they may decide to postpone the invasion indefinitely. But you look as if you didn't leave any too soon. The others?"

Dell Thompson's sun-faded eyes slitted, as if he was trying to shut out the memories that rose up before him—or endeavoring to conceal the hell that raged in their depths.

"There ain't any others—any more," he half-groaned. "They're gone—all of 'em. Jim Conklin and Asher Stewart and young Pete Calhoun—they died in hell. The spigs cut them off so that they couldn't escape, and then drove them right back into the flames. I was with Domingo Villareal. We tried to save them. I got—these." He held up his bandaged hands. "I'd have been burned to a crisp with the others, if it hadn't been for Domingo. Somehow he dragged me out of it and got me off into the brush. He died there—from his burns."

Four more gold stars to stud eternally the service flag that must always remain invisible…. Operator 5's lips moved in what might have been a benediction as he blotted out their names on the thin sheet of onion-skin that was concealed in his prescription book.

It was, as he had foreseen, practically impossible to cast suspicion upon the Japanese—but not impossible to increase the distrust with which the Orientals regarded their poorly esteemed allies. Deliberately his men were making their attempts at sabotage look like the work of Mexicans who wanted to be rid of the Asiatics.

"Fertilizer they called it, Operator 5—Japanese fertilizer, maybe!" Fidel Castro grinned when he came into the back room to have an injured eye treated. "We followed their truck train for fifty miles, and on the outside of Chinipas we came on them at night. Four truckloads of fertilizer—but when we set off timed fuses beneath them they blew the whole train to hell. There must have been more than just ammunition there—dynamite and TNT, probably. We would have gotten clear, but a carload of them coming from town cut us off. They killed Leopoldo Trevino, and we had to leave his body there."

He explained. "We tried to carry him, but Leopoldo wouldn't let us. He knew that he was dying, and he said it would be better for them to find him and see what he had in his pocket. We all carried papers in case that should happen to us—papers urging the Mexicans to arise and drive the Japs out of the country before it is stolen from them."

Leopoldo Trevino—an inconspicuous little dark-skinned man with beady black eyes. Arrogant Aryans might have disdained him—but he had served his country faithfully until death, and even after. His star would be no less brilliant than the rest....

One by one Operator 5's strange assortment of agents reported—although many of them were now only names on the reverent lips of their surviving comrades. One by one those who came in went out again to continue the grim struggle that was now increasingly difficult because Toledaro's agents were seeking them everywhere.

In the north and south, on the Atlantic coast and the Pacific, rumbles of discontent were arising; armed bands that seized towns and defied Toledaro to oust them; larger forces that fell upon federal troops and wiped out outlying garrisons. Two of those local rebellions were  assuming significant proportions—so much so that Toledaro had already publicly attributed the trouble to "the gringos from the north." His rabid newspaper statements indicated that the man was frightened, but his fear might only precipitate the invasion Jimmy Christopher was striving to prevent.

What Jimmy needed was a leader—a native leader with sufficient personality to unite the awakening people into a formidable force.

"We have succeeded in arousing our blood-brothers in Chihuahua and Sonora," Richard Wilson had brought news of Apache uprisings in the north. "They are harassing these Japanese 'farmers' so that the yellow men have turned their towns and valleys into regular military camps. But such guerrilla tactics are not sufficient to overthrow Miguel Toledaro. He is too firmly entrenched. What we need is a Pancho Villa—a man who can rally the whole country around him."

But where could such a man be found? Jimmy was mulling his

brain for a solution to that problem when another foreign-looking and queer-speaking customer arrived to have his sore throat painted. The much impressed native clerk ushered him into the back room—and Ira Hardy coughed deeply for the Mexican's benefit, while he nodded to the all-helpful Gonzalez.

"Tonight," he whispered as Jimmy soaked a swab in iodine and then tossed it into the wastebasket where the clerk would be sure to see it. "I've made the contact. They think I'm a Filipino and a red-hot anti-American; I have them eating out of my hand. Meet me at ten-thirty, and all we'll have to do is walk in and make ourselves at home. All I need is a few of those doped cigarettes." Jimmy provided the drugged cigarettes—and started to count the minutes until ten-thirty. Hardy's success was more than he had dared to hope for. It might even provide the means of frustrating the threatened invasion before it was launched! AT TEN-THIRTY he was waiting on the corner Hardy had designated, scanning each passerby until the pseudo-Filipino appeared and led the way to the Japanese Embassy.

"In here under these cherry trees," he whispered, as he invaded the embassy grounds. "There's one chap, Mabuchi, who will leave in five or ten minutes. He checks up at the telegraph station down the street, every night at this time. We'll nab him when he comes out. Then there will only be Nobumaga inside—and he should be fast asleep from the cigarette he was puffing when I just left him."

Tensely they waited until the unsuspecting Mabuchi came down the steps and appreciatively sniffed the fragrance of the blossoming trees—then something suddenly grabbed him around the legs and yanked him off his feet, while his head was engulfed in a sack that strangled him so that he could not see or make any outcry. Quickly Jimmy trussed and gagged Mabuchi, while Hardy held him securely. Then they carried him to the side of the building and dropped him into a clump of shrubbery where he would be safely disposed of until morning.

Now only Nobumaga, the watchman, remained. He had not quite succumbed to the effects of the drug he had inhaled, yet was so groggy that he toppled over backward when Hardy catapulted through the doorway. Instantly Hardy was upon him, tying him up and dragging him into an anteroom.

"Okay," he told Jimmy. "The house is yours, as promised. I'll keep watch here beside the doorway, in case His Excellence should have any more visitors this evening."

Operator 5's sharp eyes missed nothing, as he searched room after room, rifling tables and desks, breaking into closets, hunting for secret panels and wall safes—carefully putting everything back so that nobody would know it had been disturbed. In a large room, that must have served as a military council room, he found what he sought—large-scale maps on which the plans for the invasion of the United States were completely outlined!

They were cleverly conceived and worked-out plans for an invasion that could not fail! Grimly he endorsed the strategy that would over-run Texas and New Mexico, simultaneously; that would assail the weak American defense line in half a dozen places and shatter it irreparably before General Ferrara could shift his inadequate forces to bolster up the danger spots.

Cold fear trickled down Jimmy Christopher's spine, as he

visioned that plan being put into execution—the speedy and powerful mechanized Japanese columns spearing across the border, over-running all of Texas and then sweeping north and west to seize the entire Southwest and perhaps all of America west of the Mississippi! That invasion must be stopped. In some way it must be frustrated before the Japanese had a chance to realize how effectively it would work—but, meanwhile, he would take out what insurance he could against it.

Swiftly he sketched those maps and made detailed drafts of the invasion plans. At least Ferrara would have the advantage of a foreknowledge of the doom that was descending upon him.

Carefully Jimmy put the maps back in the wall cabinets exactly as he had found them, so that no alarm would cause those plans to be changed. At the door he looked back into the room to make sure that nothing was out of place, nothing disturbed so that his presence there would be suspected. Then his eyes fastened on a large oil painting hanging in the center of one of the walls—the portrait of a face he would recognize anywhere.

"Prince Saigoni—with the compliments of His Imperial Highness, Emperor Kasutosa," read the gold plate beneath it. Prince Saigoni—the suave-faced, inscrutable-eyed Eurasian whom he was getting to know so well! It was Prince Saigoni who was the personal emissary of the Mikado and the director of the Japanese operations in Mexico—and it was Prince Saigoni who had been waiting on the pier at Vera Cruz to supervise the arrest of Operator 5!

The portrait artist had succeeded admirably in capturing the half-amused, half-triumphant wraith of a smile that was the

Eurasian's outstanding characteristic. The sardonic eyes seemed to be twinkling with tolerant amusement, seemed to be waiting complacently for the certain accomplishment of aims that he knew were marching onward inexorably.

Jimmy almost felt as if Saigoni himself was gazing down from the painted canvas—and then the portrait's haunting spell was broken by a commotion downstairs in the hallway. Ira Hardy was in trouble!

SNAPPING OFF the light, Jimmy ran out into the hallway and started down the stairs. But halfway to the lower floor he saw that he was too late. Hardy was swaying on his feet, blood welling from his slashed throat and spurting from his chest—where a dagger was sunk to the hilt!

The houseboy, Mabuchi, lay dead at Hardy's feet, and two Japanese in military uniforms were worrying him like savage wolves pulling down a wounded stag—slashing and skewering him with their swords as he toppled to the floor. Ira Hardy had died at his post—but he had held his ground there, had kept on his feet with a dagger deep in his heart, long enough to give Operator 5 a warning.

Jimmy's cat-footed approach took the Japanese entirely by surprise. Before they could whirl to face him, one dropped with a leaden slug through his temple. The other made a frantic grasp for his holstered gun, but Jimmy's merciless bullet caught him squarely between the eyes.

At the foot of the stairs Jimmy raced to Hardy's sprawled body, turned it over and glanced at it once to be sure that the last breath of life had gone—and then he was at the door, peering out.

Those shots had attracted attention. There were people on the street looking at the building—men now coming toward it on the run. There wasn't a moment to spare. Quickly he blasted two wild shots at them through the shattering window of the door, then bent over Hardy to put his automatic in the dead man's hand and to snatch up Hardy's gun from the floor.

That warning blast of fire slowed up the investigators. It held them back sufficiently long so that Jimmy could race to the rear of the building, locate an exit there, then slip out through it and down a dark back alley to a side street. A few moments later he was in the clear—and the police probably were warily making their way into the embassy, to stare down at the corpses and interpret their mute story.

This intruder—who would be identified as a dog of a gringo who had posed as a Filipino—had broken into the embassy. He had been caught there and killed by the Japanese, but not before he had been able to mortally wound his discoverers. Like Leopoldo Trevino, Ira Hardy would serve even after the death he had met so unflinchingly. He would serve to cover Operator 5's tracks and dispel any suspicion that there had been another intruder who had had an opportunity to inspect those all-important maps. Also, Jimmy knew, this would have been the loyal agent's dying wish....

A job well done!

In his bedroom behind the apothecary shop Jimmy carefully prepared a letter addressed to a wholesale drug house in San

Antonio—a dummy concern whose post-office box was one of a dozen addresses he could use to contact his agents and get in touch with General Ferrara. In that envelope were several sheets of paper listing an order of supplies Luis Gonzalez needed to replenish his dwindling stock. But when those sheets were treated with the proper chemicals their reverse sides would become maps on which the plans for the Japanese invasion of America were carefully drafted.

At least that much he had been able to do, Jimmy considered as he went out and posted the letter; but it was not enough. At best, he knew, that information would only enable Ferrara to slow up the invasion that must somehow be stopped. It must be stopped before it even started….

He was still feverishly striving to find a way to do this the next day when another customer arrived with a prescription—one which went into a chemical bath as soon as Jimmy had filled it.

"Operator 5 has been condemned to death and will be shot at daybreak tomorrow morning!" stared up at him as soon as the chemicals had done their work.

Tight-lipped, Jimmy read that death sentence, and then handed the developing tray to Richard Wilson, who stood beside him. The muscles at the base of Wilson's bronzed jaws ridged out and his lean fingers hooked into talons that clenched and unclenched restlessly.

"We must get him out of there—" he started to say. But sounds outside in the shop stopped the words on his lips.

Quickly he leaned forward beside Jimmy and peered through the little glass slot which permitted a view of the outer room.

Two officers from the prison had come in and were ordering something at the counter.

Silently the watchers drew back from the slot—and when Jimmy Christopher met Wilson's gaze the Apache's dark eyes were eloquent.

CHAPTER 8
DAYBREAK OF DOOM

ANDY BRETTON had witnessed the savage murder of Juan Perez in the railroad station at Vera Cruz. He had done his best to conceal his reaction—to prevent any hint of it from showing on his set face—but the secret police who surrounded him were watching him like hawks.

"That is one less, Operator 5!" a fat, piggish faced fellow taunted. "One by one the stupid fools perish—and now that they are leaderless it will be amusing rounding up the rest of them. Or perhaps you will make the matter more simple by supplying us with a list of their names and whereabouts. That would really be advisable, unless—" He shrugged significantly at where Perez's butchered body lay in a welter of blood.

"That is an easy death—compared to some," one of his companions joined in. "We have a game here in Mexico we call 'El Gallo'. Perhaps you have not heard of it? We dig a hole deep enough to bury a man standing up—just so that his head is above ground. Then we mount horses and ride over him. There are prizes for those who snatch a tuft of his hair, an ear, an eye, perhaps a part of his nose, as they go by. It is rare sport—and

74

eventually, of course, one of the horses' hoofs comes too close to his skull. We played it for nearly an hour in Durango with your Jim Spencer when he foolishly refused to talk."

Jim Spencer had been a veteran of the Suicide Battalion that went to Europe with Operator 5. But for him Andy Bretton would not have been one of the few who came back—but Andy gave no sign of the pain that stabbed at his heart. Grim-eyed, tight-lipped, he stood their baiting until the train reached Mexico City and he was thrown into a bare cell in the grim military prison where so many prisoners entered and never came out alive.

Half a dozen times the next clay they took him before groups of Mexican officers, but he gave them no information. He did not attempt to deny that he was Operator 5, but about his companions and their objectives his lips were sealed.

Finally that procedure was varied. When he was escorted to the prison office, he found that his latest inquisitor was a plump, suave-looking man in civilian clothes. A Eurasian, Andy promptly identified him—a man in whom the facial characteristics of the East and West were curiously blended to produce a mask that was alive with little nuances of expression, little hints of what might be going on in his mind… and yet was curiously inscrutable.

"By reputation you are a very intelligent man, Operator 5—" he smiled—"but, from what I hear, you give little indication of brain capacity in your present attitude. I understand, of course, your fine scruples against betraying your men. On that score, I will not argue with you—but I offer you a compromise: call off these men, discontinue your campaign against us, give me your word that you will do nothing more to promote trouble in Mexico—and I will see that you and they are returned to the border unharmed."

"No go," Andy Bretton shook his head firmly. "In the first place, that's no bargain, and in the second place, I wouldn't trust you to keep it even if I were fool enough to accept your terms."

The Eurasian's murky eyes kindled. Hot rage leaped in their depths, but he fought it down and controlled it. For ten minutes he argued and tried to bargain, but finally, defeated, he switched his tactics and dropped his smug mask.

"Fool, I gave you a chance for your worthless life—but now you will die!" he taunted. "You do not yet know me. But very soon all of your countrymen who survive will be very well acquainted with Prince Saigoni, Regent of Mexico as soon as the new, enlarged republic becomes a protectorate under the beneficent wing of Emperor Kasutosa! The United States has lorded it over the American continents long enough. Now it will be Mexico's turn. First, the Mexican people will take back the territory that was stolen from them in eighteen-forty-five. Then, her army the greatest in the Western Hemisphere, Mexico will announce her own Monroe Doctrine that will subjugate every other American nation to her will!" He let that sink in.

"And the most amusing part of it," Saigoni chuckled, "is that your United States, by her own greed, will start this new set-up into being. Japan will have no cause for interference, as you seem to think; she will keep her pledge of non-aggression and let the

Mexican people work out their own destiny. It is unfortunate that you will not be here to watch the drama unfold, Operator 5."

The Eurasian was delighted with his secret joke. His bland smile stretched from ear to ear, and he could barely control the laughter that jiggled his near-paunch. Mockingly his chuckles rang in Andy Bretton's ears when the Mexican jailers took him back to his cell—to sit and ponder what the man could have meant....

ON THE third day, the guards paraded their prisoner to a large room where a dozen officers sat at tables arranged in a semi-circle. A court-martial Andy Bretton recognized at once. Half a dozen members of the secret police were there to quiz him—and in the background loomed the plump, suavely smiling figure of Prince Saigoni, flanked by two slant-eyed Japanese army officers.

That trial was a farce. Again the Mexicans tried every ruse to lead Andy into giving them the information they wanted, but his lips remained resolutely closed. He neither affirmed nor denied their charges, their sly implications, the words they tried to put into his mouth—and at last they gave up and accepted defeat.

"Operator 5, it is the judgment of this military tribunal that you are guilty of fostering widespread espionage, of attempting to overthrow the government of the Republic of Mexico, of overt acts against the government and of murdering its citizens," the general who presided over the court proclaimed. "The penalty for these high crimes is death—and we therefore sentence you to be shot at daybreak tomorrow morning."

Boxed in by his guards, Andy Bretton started back to his

cell—and with him went the memory of a placid moon-face that was wreathed in a triumphant, mocking smile.

This was the end, he knew—the end when it should be but the beginning. For now he knew the identity of the man whose ominous threat hung over America; now he had information that should be rushed to Operator 5 without delay. It *must* be gotten to him….

Like an automaton, a man stunned by the fate that had over-taken him, Andy marched along—but suddenly he faltered and seemed to turn his ankle. To one side he lurched, halfway to one knee—and then he was diving straight ahead of him, using his handcuffed hands as a flail. One of the soldier guards went down under that charge. His rifle clattered to the stone floor, and Andy dived for it. But another gun butt slapped against the side of his head, and he spun dizzily across the corridor, to collapse in a heap against a cell door as they piled on top of him.

Stunned and weak in the knees, he lay there staring up at a provokingly familiar face that peered at him from behind the bars—a haggard, bearded face that he ought to know. Then they yanked him to his feet and dragged him back to his cell.

He had had little hope of succeeding in that frantic effort—and yet its failure added to his desperation. In some way he *had* to get out of that cell. Somehow, he *had* to reach Operator 5! But now there was a sentry posted in front of his cell door—a sentry who stolidly resisted all his offers and blandishments, and who wisely kept well out of reach. That sounded the knell of Andy's last hope.

That last night was a ghastly ordeal. Hour after hour slipped by—and with each passing minute his chance of being able to contact anyone on the outside grew more slim. Saigoni, he realized, had been diabolically clever in those taunting revelations. Deliberately, he had supplied information which he knew would rankle in the prisoner's mind and add to his torture in those last fleeting hours.

Hour after hour… while Andy tried to drive his thought into other, saner channels—tried to identify that curiously familiar face that had peered out at him from between the bars. But the man's personality eluded him… and then the stone corridor echoed with the tramp of feet, and a squad of soldiers marched up to relieve the yawning guard!

One of the Mexicans unlocked the cell door, pushed it open. Andy Bretton squared his shoulders and, with eyes straight ahead of him, walked out to meet his doom.

Into the barren quadrangle that was the center of the prison they marched him—over to a blank stone wall pitted and scarred with the marks of hundreds of bullets. It was considerably after daybreak, he noticed—but probably that was to be expected of people to whom promptness, even in death, meant nothing. The sun was well up—was flashing on the shining blade of the officer's drawn sword.

Flashing and blinking—*in the Morse code!*

Incredulously, Andy stared, but there *it* was, unmistakably: letter after letter—*D-r-o p!*

The officer's voice snapped a command, and eight rifles rose to shoulders; another command, and eight dark-skinned fingers tightened on triggers. The sword was raised high.

"Fire!"

The blade flashed down, and the gun roared—and Andy Bretton swayed, twisted crazily on one leg, and fell facedown in the dirt—even though no bullet had pierced his body!

TENSE, HOLDING his breath so that no slightest movement of his body would betray that he still lived, he lay there and waited for he knew not what. Now the officer was bending over him, looking down at him—and Andy felt something wet splash on his face and spill on the ground. Something red that looked like blood, he glimpsed through eyelids that were parted only the barest fraction of an inch.

Again the officer's voice crackled sharp commands, and the execution squad shouldered their rifles and marched out of the quadrangle.

For what seemed hours, Andy lay there, not daring to move a muscle. Then once more he heard the pound of feet, saw two figures approaching him. On the ground beside him they dropped a tarpaulin, and rolled him up in it. He could feel the tarpaulin leave the ground; could feel himself being carried, dropped down with a jolt—and when the tarpaulin was unrolled he stared up into the faces of Operator 5 and Hugh Delcourt's Apache, Richard Wilson!

"Quick—get out of those clothes and into this uniform," Jimmy Christopher snapped, as he held out a Mexican private's outfit, replete with rifle and an additional automatic. "No questions now—they may be in on us at any moment."

"It's no question," Andy Bretton whispered excitedly as he made a switch of clothing that would have won the envy of a quick-change artist. "Hugh Delcourt is here in this prison! I saw him yesterday afternoon and couldn't place him—but seeing Wilson just now jogged my memory. Delcourt is in a cell at the other end of the corridor where they kept me."

"Hugh Delcourt!" Operator 5's eyes snapped as he turned to the grim-faced Apache. "We can't leave him here. We'll take him along!" he decided quickly. "First let's locate the turnkey."

With the newly made private trailing a few paces in their rear, those two who seemed to be Mexican officers left the storeroom where Andy Bretton had come back to life. They marched across the deserted quadrangle to the corridor from which Operator 5 had supposedly gone forth to his death. With cautious deliberateness, they walked down the corridor toward the office where the turnkey should be peacefully dozing.

Jimmy's hand was ready on the hilt of his sword as he stepped into the open doorway, but the room was empty—and then they caught the sound of nasal laughter from the guard-room next door.

"That's the fellow!" Andy whispered. "I'd know that laugh anywhere in God's world!"

Jimmy's eyes clouded. There were other voices coming from the guard-room—half a dozen of them, at least. Perhaps the entire execution squad were in there—which would make the odds three to one. But he remembered that day when Hugh Delcourt rode out from Santa Fe and pledged him the support of every man in the Southwest who could aim a gun....

"We'll have to work fast—and silently," he reminded them. "I'll go in first, with you right at my heels. We should be in the midst of them before they realize anything is wrong—and then it will be too late."

Unsheathing his sword, he grasped the doorknob and stepped

THE DAY OF THE DAMNED

In an instant the guardroom became
a slaughter-house, a shambles!

inside, to be greeted by startled glances from the lounging soldiers. Shamefacedly, half-angrily, they started to get to their feet—when suddenly a shout of surprise came from one corner of the room.

"That's not Captain Rogaz!" one of the men yelled. "I thought he looked strange before—and now I understand. That's Captain Rogaz' uniform he's wearing—I can tell by that stain on the sleeve—but he's a fake!"

His rifle was in his hands, lowered threateningly, as he came charging forward. But Jimmy leaped in with split-second speed and brushed the weapon aside, to run the fellow through with his sword. In an instant the guard-room became a slaughterhouse, a shambles. The surprised soldiers grabbed for their rifles—only to find two swords flashing deadly lightning in front of their eyes, while a madman, with a long knife that dripped blood was all over the room at once.

The moment he stepped through the doorway, Richard Wilson had thrust his sword into Andy Bretton's hand and unsheathed the keen-bladed Apache knife that was hidden beneath his uniform. Silently that terrible weapon worked, but so effectively that it stretched three of the Mexicans lifeless on the floor before they could do so much as shout for help. Two others had gone down under those flashing sword-blades—and then the turnkey, making a desperate dash for the door, pitched forward with that bone-handled Indian knife quivering in the base of his brain!

That was too much for the cowed survivors. They threw down their rifles and dropped to their knees as they begged for mercy.

Quickly they were disarmed, bound and gagged; and then Andy Bretton, with the keeper's keys led the way to Hugh Delcourt's cell.

"Operator 5!" the amazed governor exclaimed when he recognized his rescuer. "And you, Richard! Then Davie did manage to reach you, Operator 5! I was so afraid, after he had gone, that I had sent him to his death!"

Jimmy Christopher's heart constricted as he looked at his old friend, and he could not tell him of his son's death. Delcourt's husky figure was shrunken, his nearly two hundred pounds reduced to little more than half that weight. His unshaven cheeks were gaunt, and his eyes were deep-sunken—but they were still bright and undaunted.

"They have me chained to the bars." He pointed to the heavy manacles that held him when Jimmy tried to urge him from the cell.

ANDY BRETTON went to work again with the big ring of keys, and while he tried to find the one that would fit the rusty lock Jimmy quickly outlined for the old man what had happened—sketched the developments in Mexico and what he had discovered about Saigoni.

"Revolution is the only answer," Delcourt nodded vigorously, "For that you need a leader—and he is right here in our hands. Avila Morelos is in a cell just around that next corner. Take him out of here with us and you will have Toledaro trembling in his palace!"

Avila Morelos, the young revolutionary chieftain who had been Toledaro's chief rival! The descendant of one of Mexico's revolutionary heroes, he was just the man Operator 5 needed to consolidate popular support behind the sporadic rebellions his men were fanning into life!

As soon as Hugh Delcourt was free he started on a run for Avila Morelos' cell, clasped the bars and hoarsely whispered the good news to the prisoner, while Andy Bretton found the right key and unlocked the door. The handsome young Mexican's eyes flashed with excitement as he strode out from the bars and clasped the hands of his deliverers.

"Gracias, amigos!" he whispered. "This day I am in your debt—but soon it may be given to me to repay you!"

Back through the winding corridors toward the big front gate Jimmy Christopher led the way. Only silence greeted them. Apparently their escape had not been discovered—until suddenly his keen eyes caught a flicker of sunlight on the barrel of a gun.

"Down!" he shouted, just as a volley of lead poured into the corridor from one of the entrances to the quadrangle.

Back on their feet, the uninjured fugitives hotfooted it for the gate—and the safety of the car that waited for them outside the prison. But now the corridors were ringing with shouts and orders. Soldiers were running from every direction, trying to cut them off; bullets were seeking them, slapping against the walls and ricocheting crazily as they glanced off stone pillars.

They seemed to have charmed lives as they raced out of the building and made a dash for the heavy gate in the adobe wall that surrounded the prison—but one of those wild ricochets had hit Hugh Delcourt. He was limping badly, barely able to keep on his feet.

There were two soldiers on guard at the gate, but Jimmy and Andy Bretton shot them down—only to have a dozen more come running from the prison doorway they had just left. Behind those were more—the whole garrison was now turning out.

Through that gateway Andy Bretton and Richard Wilson plunged, Jimmy Christopher and Hugh Delcourt close behind them—but just at the portal the old man's wounded leg seemed to give way beneath him. He pitched to one side and grasped at the heavy gate. Jimmy whirled, tried to spring to his aid—but the metal gate clanged shut and was barred from the inside… where Hugh Delcourt stood backed against it, his guns blazing!

"Go on—for God's sake, go on!" he shouted above the din. "We can't all make it—someone has to stay and hold these rats in their trap. That's my job—all I'm good for now. The safety of America depends on you, Operator 5! You can't fail—"

A perfect thunder of rifle fire drowned out his voice, but then it rose again—and Operator 5 felt an agonizing lump rise in his throat as a gasping, "God bless you!" speeded him on his way. Barely had he flung himself into the rear of the car beside Avila Morelos when the gate swung open—but those few moments which Hugh Delcourt had bought so dearly were all they needed to spurt away from the curb and speed to safety.

There, more than a thousand miles from the Santa Fe he loved so well, another fearless son of the Southwest had joined the glorious company of her immortals….

CHAPTER 9
FILIBUSTER'S RED
RENDEZVOUS!

DIANE ELLIOT was fully conscious long before the plane in which she was a captive made a landing. Frantically, she had been working on the ropes that bound her wrists, trusting that the noise of the engine would cover any sounds she was forced to make. But the ropes were tightly bound. Her wrists were raw and bleeding before she had made any progress—and her hands were not free until the plane bumped to a landing on a field that was illuminated by a single light.

Perfectly still she lay on the floor and blinked up with dazed appearing eyes when the ship's ceiling light flashed on—but the moment her captor bent over to pick her up she flew at him desperately. With all her strength she tried to pull him down, to get a grip on his throat—but all she succeeded in doing was tearing the mask from his face. Then his arms were around her, twisting her hands behind her back and holding her.

"A little spitfire, eh?" he chuckled. "Good, I like spunk—this promises to make you much more interesting!" And when she caught a glimpse of his eyes she read frank admiration in their depths.

His face was handsome, in a bold, dashing sort of way; the face of a big, strong man, arrogant and masterful. A face that she knew she should recognize—but his identity eluded her.

Easily he lifted her from the plane and carried her through the faintly starlit darkness to what she identified as a low, sprawling ranch-house. Its front half was built of wood, but the rear was adobe, and into that section he bore her—to set her down in a small, barely furnished room with a stoutly barred window that looked out into the night.

The place was a cell as impregnable as those in any prison.

"Sorry I can't offer you more luxurious accommodations, Miss Elliot," he grinned, "but you will understand, I have to take some—er—precautions. *Buenos noches,* until the morning!"

So he knew her identity, Diane considered as she sank down on the made-up cot, after the lock had clicked in that stout metal reinforced door. He probably knew it all along, knew that she was one of Operator 5's agents—which was why she had been shadowed so carefully. That meant that the plans she had overheard must be approaching a climax. They would hold her here until their invasion was underway, until she could no longer interfere with it—but she must find some way to stop it! In some way she *must* get out of that place so that she could convey her news to Jimmy!

Far into the night she wrestled with that problem, but at last sleep overcame her—and held her far later the next morning than she intended. It was a tapping on her door that awakened her, the soft voice of an old Mexican woman bearing a tray of food. Diane tried to question her, but the crone shrugged her shoulders and pretended not to understand anything.

It was some hours later before her kidnaper came to call. In the light of day the familiarity of his boldly handsome face was even more striking than on the night before.

"Who are you?" she asked him frankly, after a few minutes of conversational sparring. "I know why you brought me here—but I don't know who you are, though something about your face tells me that I should."

But he merely shrugged. "What does it matter?" he laughed. "Who I am now is of no importance—it is what I am going to be that matters."

Again she saw the open admiration in his eyes—and played up to it as adroitly as she could.

"You must be someone of importance already, or else your face would not be so familiar to me," she eyed him archly. "I know something about character reading. I can see that you are accustomed to command—that you are a leader of men. I heard sufficient at that window in New Orleans last night to have a very good idea of what is afoot—and that sounds to me very much like your work. Joab Burley seemed to be their leader—but you do not look to me like the sort of man who will take orders from anyone else. You are nobody's hireling."

The grin on his face widened, and she could see that he was pleased.

"You're not bad—for a girl," he admitted, with new respect in his tone, "and I'm glad I picked you up last night. You are lots safer here where I can keep an eye on you—and where you can't put ideas in anyone else's head. You're right—this is my ranch, and I take orders from nobody here. You will see plenty of men arriving; all members of my outfit—all getting ready for the drive that will carry us to Mexico City before Miguel Toledaro has a chance to call out his guard!" He studied her.

"The Mexican people are fed up with Japanese infiltration

and domination," he warmed to his subject. "All of Northern Mexico is ripe for revolt. I am going to lead the army of liberation—and when the fighting is over, *I* will be the master of one of the strongest nations on the American continents. Not the president—no, Joab Burley can have that high-sounding title. But I will be the *dictator*, the one who will pull the strings that will control the destiny of the Western Hemisphere!"

The man had a power complex, Diane realized as she listened to him and saw the fanatical gleam in his eyes—he was half-mad on the subject. But it would be worse than useless to seem to oppose him now.

"A man who can control the destiny of the whole Western hemisphere!" she repeated softly, raptly. "I have often thought that that is our only hope—our only hope of escaping from being gobbled up by the dictators of Europe or Asia. Emperor Rudolph almost succeeded. The next time we will not be able to throw off the yoke—unless a man arises who is so strong that he can dominate and unite all the countries of the Western hemisphere; a man so strong that no dictator will dare to attack him!"

As if unconsciously, her hand reached out and fastened on his.

"Somehow," she murmured softly, "you inspire me with confidence. Somehow, you make me feel that *you* are such a man—but I do not even know your name!" she broke off suddenly.

"You will know it," he promised as he rose and strode to the window. "But now I am needed outside. Some of my men are arriving."

A DOZEN riders were approaching the ranch, she saw from the window after he had left. All that day they kept arriving, and even more when night screened their movements. Day by day their number increased and the store of military equipment that was arriving piled higher and higher. Day by day Diane flirted with her captor, used her every wile upon him in a desperate hope that she would find some way to gain the upper hand and thwart his mad project before it was too late. But he was no fool. Even in his most zealous moments he was wary and on guard.

"You are very lovely, Diane," he told her frankly. "You are the sort of partner I always dreamed of having—but I can't afford to lose my head. I can't afford to take the slightest chance with you until I know that anything you might do can no longer stop us. It will only be a little while longer; our day is almost at hand." That day came all too swiftly. It was to be a sort of dress rehearsal for the defense units that were organized all through the Southwest, a "concentration" along the border—actually, a pretext which would allow the filibusters to launch their thrust into Mexico.

"We will be ready in half an hour," he told her when he came to her cellroom, all caparisoned in his olive-green uniform. "There is only one doubt in my mind—and that is whether or not to take you with us. You say you want to go, but there may be danger—"

At that moment a horse screamed wildly and men's voices rose in excited shouts. Diane's captor stepped to the window to see what had happened—and she saw the chance for which she had been so patiently waiting! Stepping up behind him, she reached out and plucked the heavy revolver from the holster on his hip—and brought it down over his skull before he had a chance to whirl and seize her!

For an instant his eyes stared at her reproachfully—then they closed and his big frame sagged, toppled to the floor in a limp sprawl. Quickly Diane snatched the twin weapon from his other holster, concealed it in the blouse of the khaki riding outfit with which he had provided her, and stepped out of the room, locking the door behind her.

Carefully she made her way down the corridor, eyes and ears tense and alert for the first sign of danger. Now that she was free, she must find a way out of this place—an exit by which she could slip off unobserved and put miles behind her before her escape was discovered.

That corridor joined another which led toward the rear of the building. Diane started along it, and suddenly was electrified by the sound of a voice—Tim Donovan's voice coming from behind the closed door beside her!

Revolver held ready in her hand, she waited tensely until that door opened and the old serving woman backed out—only to drop her tray and stiffen like a ramrod when the gun barrel jabbed against the back of her neck. Into the room she was pushed. And before Diane had the door closed, Tim was up from his cot and had the old Mexican on the floor stopping her mouth with a towel gag, holding her helpless while Diane ripped her voluminous skirt and petticoats to shreds and tied her up with the strips.

"Diane!" Tim exulted jubilantly. "I've been praying for a miracle—but I didn't expect an angel to come to my rescue!"

"A very pretty speech, young man," Diane smiled as she finished tying up her former jailer; "almost as pretty as those I've been listening to for the past week from the big Adonis who seems to run this place."

"That must be Sam Blankenship," Tim explained, "Governor Hugh Delcourt's adjutant and right-hand man. He has been pulling the wool over the old man's eyes by organizing defense battalions all through the Southwest, as camouflage for a crack-brained filibuster scheme of his own."

Sam Blankenship… immediately Diane recalled newspaper stories of the soldier-of-fortune's exploits and realized why the man's face had been so familiar. With Sam Blankenship directing it, this filibuster expedition was doubly dangerous—must be brought to the attention of Operator 5 at the earliest possible moment.

QUICKLY SHE and Tim compared notes and made hurried plans. Locking the old woman in Tim's cell, they continued cautiously down the corridor to the rear door. It opened onto a sunbaked stretch that led to a corral where fifty or sixty horses ran free. But at the edge of the enclosure was a stunted live-oak tree, with half a dozen saddled animals tied to its trunk.

"There's our answer," Tim whispered. "It will be too risky to hunt around for a car, but I can get a couple of those mounts."

Leisurely he walked to the live-oak and unhitched two of the best looking animals, walked them back to where Diane waited and helped her into the saddle. Apparently they had not been observed, but now would come the test. Unhurriedly they started away from the house, toward a trail that led away from the rear—but almost instantly a gruff voice shouted a suspicious challenge after them.

"Now let's see what these crowbaits can do," Tim cried as he quirted his horse and flung himself close over its neck.

They had a start, but soon a score of riders were on their trail. Some of those horses were fast—they began to cut down the distance—and now the pursuers were yelling threats.

"Stop or we'll bring you down!" one of them howled.

Tim's freckled face became a taut mask, as he pressed closer to the animal's mane and turned anxious eyes to where Diane's slower-footed animal was beginning to lag. Now a rattle of gunfire had broken out behind them. Bullets were falling short, but it would not be long before they were within range. Diane realized that, too. Her face was set, eyes wide and desperate—only to flood with dismay when her mount screamed shrilly and leaped into the air.

One of those bullets had caught him in the flank; not a disabling wound, but it slowed him up—and now it would be only a question of minutes before they brought him down. He was almost lame when they reached the top of a little rise, and there Diane flung herself from the saddle, forced the animal to lie down and crouched low behind him.

"Go on—go on, Tim!" she begged, when he reined in his animal and rode back to her. "Someone has to reach Jimmy or General Ferrara with the news in time to prevent these fools from plunging us into a war! An invasion is just what the Japanese want—it will be the end of America. You have to stop that, Tim!"

"But, Di—I can't leave you here like this," Tim groaned. "Jimmy wouldn't—"

"Jimmy Christopher would expect you to do your duty!" Diane snapped, as her revolver barked a warning shot at the approaching riders. "You know what he would do if he were here. I'll hold this gang off as long as I can—but *please* don't waste any more time!"

Tim Donovan did know what Jimmy Christopher would do under the circumstances; he understood the uncompromising devotion to duty that motivated the man his countrymen knew as Operator 5. Not even the life of this girl, which was far more precious to him than his own existence, would have swayed Jimmy when the fate of America hung in the balance. The path of duty was stern and unrelenting—and Tim took it.

"See you in El Paso, Di!" he choked—and then he was urging his horse along the trail, as he fought back the mist that blurred his eyes.

Flat on the ground behind the wounded horse, Diane Elliot blazed away at the oncoming horsemen. Two of the mounts went down and spilled their riders headlong. But now the pack was dividing, circling around her on both sides. She had only six cartridges that had been in Sam Blankenship's gun; the other she had given to Tim.

The moment her last shot was fired they seemed to sense that her gun was empty and that she had no other ammunition. From all sides they closed in and overwhelmed her. Helpless on the wounded horse, surrounded on every side by angry-faced riders who were furious that half their quarry had escaped, she rode back toward the ranch.

Before they reached it Sam Blankenship came spurring along the trail. His face was bleak with rage when he heard that Tim Donovan had escaped—but gradually his anger cooled and he shrugged.

"It will make no difference," he assured Diane. "By the time he reaches Ferrara it will be too late—we are already moving!"

IMPATIENTLY TIM DONOVAN spurred and quirted his mount as he made a bee-line in what he thought must be the direction of El Paso. But the border city was at least a hundred miles away, as well as he was able to figure—and he did not dare to stop at the scattered ranches he passed for fear the occupants might be members of Blankenship's outfit, which had drawn heavily on this section of the country.

As soon as Diane had heard of Jimmy's plan to enter Mexico with his undercover legion, she had agreed that it would be too risky to return to Santa Fe in hope of finding him. In all probability he had already left—and now the only one who might be able to check Blankenship and Joab Burley was Sylvester Ferrara.

Tim's horse was nearly foundered by the time he managed to commandeer a small car at gun point. Docilely the scared driver turned around and headed for El Paso. But the machine was an ancient wreck. There was constant trouble with it, until Tim almost wished that he had stuck to his jaded horse—but at last they chugged into the outskirts of the city and located General Ferrara's headquarters.

Ferrara was at the newly constructed military airport, his aide reported; he was bidding farewell to his fellow—Triumvir, Joab Burley!

Tim reached that field at top speed, and even from the distance he could see that Burley's plane was all ready to take to the air—that Ferrara was standing beside it, shaking hands with Burley in the doorway!

"Wait a minute, General!" Tim shouted frantically, as he raced across the field. "Hold that plane!"

Ferrara turned in amazement—and then Tim was beside him, was panting out the story of Blankenship's treachery and the impending invasion of Mexico—was exposing Burley's connection with it.

"You can't let Burley get away from here, General!" he urged desperately, as Ferrara hesitated with apparent uncertainty. "He is the head of the outfit. One of the Triumvirs of the United States leading an armed invasion of Mexico—that will mean war—will mean that we will be overrun by the Japanese!"

Joab Burley's florid face had become crimson. His eyes narrowed and his lips tightened. Suddenly an automatic was gripped in his hand, pointing straight at Sylvester Ferrara's heart.

"Hands off, Ferrara!" he ordered. "If you, or anyone else, tries to stop me I'll kill you! All right, Lopez," he called to the pilot—and the motor roared; the ship began to move.

Before anyone could attempt to interfere, the cabin door snapped shut and the ship sped down the field and zoomed into the air. For a moment Ferrara watched as it cleared the ground; watched and hoped against hope that Tim Donovan might be wrong—but the plane headed *south*, into Mexico, and the hostilities Operator 5 had struggled so desperately to prevent were about to be precipitated!

CHAPTER 10
BURNED OFFERING

AS THE fleeing car sped out of Mexico City, Andy Bretton recounted what he had learned from the lips of Prince Saigoni and Jimmy Christopher began to understand the subtlety of the sly game the wily Eurasian was playing. Holding out half of the United States as bait to Toledaro, he was tricking the Mexican president into enslaving his nation to Japan.

But now his treacherous scheme would be thwarted!

As Avila Morelos listened to that revealing recital, his dark eyes glowed with rage. He restlessly fingered the automatic Jimmy had given him as he left his cell. Added to his disdain for Miguel Toledaro was a growing hatred for these Orientals who were over-running the land.

"My ancestors suffered greatly to free Mexico from beneath the heel of the Spanish oppressors, and now this scurvy dog would surrender our hard-won liberties to these alien Japanese!" he said softly. "But he shall not succeed—I swear it by all the saints! Our people will rise and free the country of Toledaro and all his yellow-skinned friends!"

Desperately the Mexicans tried to stop that fleeing car. Twice barricades waited for it as the fugitives roared through towns on their way north. But the heavy Packard had been well chosen.

It snapped the stretched wires and battered its way through the piled-up barrels and planks, while from its windows the defenders poured a deadly fire into the ambushed police and soldiers, who had been notified by telegraph to stop them.

Twice they broke through, and after that the efforts to stop them became only half-hearted. Now the car was speeding through Avila Morelos' own country. Crowds cheered him in the village streets, when he waved to them from the window—and by the time they reached San Luis Potosi, Morelos' native city, a small-size army was waiting to greet him.

Operator 5's agents had been at work in that territory, and now it needed but the sight of Morelos' smiling face and waving hand to send the populace into a frenzy. Overnight, an army flocked to his revolutionary banner—an army that increased hourly as it swept eastward toward the vital east coast oil fields.

Hastily Toledaro rushed government troops to stop him. But one contingent was ambushed and annihilated, when their leader foolishly walked them into the trap Morelos had made of the village of San Barto. Another force Morelos routed disastrously near Espinazo, and his successes quickly brought other chieftains with their guerrilla bands flocking to join him.

Down the valley of the Verde River the triumphant revolutionists swept, through the low coastal range until they reached the Verde's confluence with the Panuco—and then the wide coastal plain and the richest oil region in Mexico lay before them.

Panic-stricken, Toledaro hurled every available man into the breach to check that irresistible tide. When Jimmy's agents had succeeded in wiping out almost the entire Western coast oil district around Tehuantepec, Toledaro had trebled his garrisons around the Eastern fields and had been guarding them carefully, so as to insure an oil supply for his Japanese allies—but now he rushed fresh troops into the vital sector.

Steadily the federal forces were pushed backward, until Morelos was at the very gates of Tampico.

"Tomorrow morning we will go forward—and by tomorrow night the city will be completely in our hands," he exulted, as the last of the government outposts were sent fleeing into the city's last line of defense.

But before morning the situation had changed rapidly—on the verge of overwhelming victory, the revolutionists suddenly found themselves threatened with crushing defeat. During the night, Toledaro and his staff had rushed a mechanized force of Japanese southeastward through the state of Tamaulipas; had brought them up in the rear of Morelos' forces, partially encircling them, so that the revolutionists were trapped. Caught in the jaws of a pincers, the Japanese at their rear and the Mexicans in front of them, the revolutionists had no choice but to go forward or be annihilated in the deadly crossfire that was inevitable.

"That is what they want us to do—go forward," Morelos worried as his staff gathered in his tent just before dawn. "They have a trap for us and the Japanese will push us into it so that there will be no turning back. But we have no choice."

"Perhaps," Operator 5 nodded, "but if I can get word into the city we may still have another card up our sleeves."

At San Luis Potosi, Jimmy had rallied as many of his agents as were within reach. Under the command of Andy Bretton, they had gone down to the coast and worked their way into Tampico, while Jimmy stayed with the revolutionist chieftain. Since that time, there had been no word from Bretton, no indication whether he and his men were alive or dead. But now Jimmy had to know—had to gamble that at least some of them had survived.

There was still time, he noticed as he left the staff conference. Dawn was just beginning to gray the sky, but the darkness was still sufficient for his purpose. Hurrying to the crest of a hill that had been wrested from the government troops in the previous day's fighting, he set up a magnesium beacon, worked over it a few moments, and a bright red flare stabbed up at the dark heavens. That flame would be visible for miles around and could easily be seen from the heart of Tampico—and Andy Bretton was an expert in reading its Morse code messages.

Operating the cup-shaped lid that fitted tightly over the beacon, Jimmy sent forth his coded call for help.

"Attacking at eight-thirty this morning," he flashed.

"Fear a trap. Any diversion of enemy forces will be invaluable."

Three times he repeated that message, and could only hope that watchful eyes would be on the lookout to take it down and decode it….

AT EIGHT-THIRTY Avila Morelos gave the word, and the first wave of his troops swept forward. With the first sound of their firing, the onslaught from the rear commenced, but the revolutionists were prepared for this, and able to hold it in check. The danger spot was ahead, in that No Man's Land on the outskirts of Tampico—and when the advancing line was well into danger territory Morelos' fears were realized.

With a thunderous roar the very ground opened up and rose toward heaven in a fearful, man-made earthquake! Earth and stones mingled with the grisly remnants of human bodies in the ghastly hail that pelted back upon the torn ground. Where a moment before there had been nearly a thousand eager, on-rushing patriots, there was now only the silence of death and the agonized cries of those mangled sufferers who had not had the good fortune to die instantly.

The terrible carnage of that deadly mine spread panic through the ranks of the Morelistas. Half-demoralized, they awaited the crushing attack that must come at any moment—when suddenly the earth trembled again in a series of terrific explosions that were like the reports of gargantuan cannon crackers with which the gods might have played!

From the hillock that was Morelos' headquarters, Jimmy Christopher peered through field glasses and saw the blinding sheets of flame, the shower of fragments hurled high in the air. He saw the great black clouds that billowed up from the heart of Tampico—and then the raging inferno that spread over the city as if liquid was surging through its streets.

For more than fifteen minutes, the earth shook beneath those rumbling blasts as the great oil tanks exploded when the flames reached them—and by that time Morelos' cheering troops had carried everything before them. Floundering almost knee-deep over the torn ground, where their comrades had been blown to

The defenders were fleeing in a wild panic from the inferno creeping up on them!

atoms, the revolutionists swept into the government entrenchments, from which the defenders were already fleeing in wild
panic before the inferno that was creeping up on them from
the rear.

Stunned and utterly disorganized by the catastrophe that had
befallen them, they surrendered by the thousands, threw down
their arms and begged for mercy—and the way into blazing
Tampico was open. Grimly the Morelistas wiped out the last
semblance of resistance and then streamed into the ruins of one
of the world's greatest oil ports.

"Those explosions were Heaven-sent!" Avila Morelos vowed
piously. "The Heavenly Father came to our aid in the moment
of our greatest need! He has sounded the doom of Toledaro and
his heathen allies!"

But Jimmy Christopher knew that if the dynamiting of those
huge oil tanks was the work of Providence it had been accomplished through the medium of Andy Bretton and a dozen hardy
souls who must have applied the matches to the fuses—and
Andy and his comrades were there somewhere in the raging
furnace that had been a great city....

Braving the heat and the flames as far as was humanly possible, Jimmy ventured into the gutted streets with the advance
patrols. Hopefully he scrutinized each group of prisoners that
was brought in, but nowhere was there a sign of any of his
men—until he almost stumbled over a charred and blistered
mummy that crawled out of a doorway and called after him.

Instantly he was at the side of that horribly burned figure, holding the blistered hand, staring into the almost unrecognizable face and listening to the croaking voice of John Two Eagles.

"We caught your message," the Indian gasped. "We were waiting and watching day and night. We had made our contacts, had access to the wells and refineries. Everything was in readiness but the fuses—they were not in place. There was no time—so we did not use them."

"You set off those tanks without fuses!" Jimmy gasped. "Andy Bretton—where is he?"

"Where does the soul go when it leaves the body?" The Apache's eyes were glazing. "He set off one of the first tanks—he had no chance to escape. They are gone, Operator 5—all are gone—and now I shall join them. Now...."

Death stilled the blistered lips, and the singed eyelids closed. John Two Eagles had gone to that abode of his forefathers where the soul goes when it leaves the body. And as Jimmy Christopher knelt beside the seared corpse, face after face flashed in review through his mind—a gallant company who had unhesitatingly followed loyal, dependable Andy Bretton into the very jaws of flaming hell!

With an aching heart Jimmy rose and stared at the blazing holocaust that was Andy Bretton's funeral pyre. But at least, he consoled himself, Andy had not died in vain. Tampico and its vital oil fields were lost to Prince Saigoni, and now the way was open for Morelos to sweep down the coast to Vera Cruz and then to close in on Mexico City. The threat to America had been nipped in the bud....

A GAY party gathered in Avila Morelos' headquarters that

night to celebrate the victory. Forgotten in the flush of success were the comrades who had given their lives to insure that triumph. Their exultant fellows could see only tomorrow and the success that was inevitable.

"To the new President of the Republic of Mexico—Avila Morelos!" shouted one of his officers. But even as glasses were held high to drink the toast an orderly appeared at the door to announce the receipt of a telegraph message from the north.

"Mexico has been invaded!" he proclaimed. "An American army under the personal command of Triumvir Joab Burley has crossed the border and is sweeping down through Chihuahua!"

That news came like a bombshell. The raised glasses lowered uncertainly, and every eye turned to where Operator 5 stood, too stunned to fully comprehend what had happened. For a long moment there was absolute, drama-tense silence—while Morelos' handsome face darkened and his eyes clouded with mounting rage.

"Treachery!" he gritted. "We have been tricked, played with like stupid fools! While you were busy causing turmoil in the interior of Mexico, your compatriots were gathered at the border, waiting for an opportunity to start their invasion. Our victory today, which shattered the government army, was the signal that released them—but they will not succeed! Now that Mexican territory has been violated there is no more room for internal disputes. Every Mexican soldier marches north! Rodriguez—" he turned to his chief-of-staff—"give the orders! We march to repel the invaders in the morning!"

In that bitter moment Jimmy Christopher realized what

Prince Saigoni had meant when he told Andy Bretton that American greed would pave the way for the nation's downfall. The crafty Eurasian had very carefully maneuvered all this—had traded upon Joab Burley's lust for power and then tricked the bombastic fool into invading Mexico. Now Saigoni would pour his Japanese troops across the Rio Grande—and claim that they were Mexican farmers defending their homes!

The invasion of America was inevitable, without even the necessity for a declaration of war....

CHAPTER 11
DEATH'S TOWN

FROM ALL sections of the Southwest, Sam Blankenship's defense battalions headed for the Mexican border on the day of their "concentration." Light artillery, armored cars, whippet tanks, swift-mounted cavalry troops—each went to its assigned place; and toward Deming, New Mexico, converged the crack units. By noon of the day of the dress rehearsal, Deming's wide main street was cluttered with the mobile impedimenta of a modern army, while nearly a thousand tight-lipped, earnest-eyed filibusters jammed the town and waited for the word to advance.

Closely guarded in one of those armored cars rode Diane Elliot, under the watchful eyes of two guards Blankenship had assigned to guard her. Vainly she pleaded with them, but they turned a deaf ear to her appeals. When she tried to trick them, they were alert, threatened to handcuff her unless she behaved.

"You are fools—blind fools!" she berated them. "I don't know what you think you will accomplish by this mad expedition, but I know what you are doing—you are betraying America into the hands of the Japanese!"

"Don't worry about that, Miss—we'll handle the slant-eyes," they laughingly assured her; and beyond that she could not get.

As soon as Blankenship reached Deming he went into a brief consultation with his chief lieutenants, gave his outfit a final inspection—and then issued the order to march thirty miles south to Columbus, just above the border. There the defense battalions had already relieved General Ferrara's regular troops in the newly constructed entrenchments, and were going through the invasion-repelling drills they had been practicing—when, to their amazement, a heavily armed column crept up on them not from the south, but from the *north!*

Totally unprepared for any such part of the program, they gaped helplessly into the muzzles of the unlimbered machine-guns that first covered, then cleared them out of the way. Wonderingly, they stood aside and watched in astonishment as that grimly capable-looking column swept on right over the border into Chihuahua! Watched as a grinning, whooping band of Mexican irregulars came riding out of the chaparral to greet the invaders with enthusiasm!

With machine-like precision that invasion was launched, and before the officers of the defense battalions were liberated and could communicate with headquarters at El Paso it was too late—Blankenship's invaders were hidden behind a cloud of dust that was setting in the distant south.

Almost without opposition, that column swept through the northern part of Chihuahua. Town after town surrendered without the firing of a shot, and constantly the number of their Mexican allies increased.

When the opposition did develop, it was wiped out ruthlessly—and it was the Mexicans who led the assault and reveled in the carnage.

"*Viva* Burley!" they shouted. "Down with Toledaro!"

Like wild butchers they shot and hewed their way through the opposing force, and before they were satisfied the town that had been the scene of the resistance was a flaming shambles.

"There was no occasion for such slaughter!" Diane protested as soon as she was able to locate Blankenship. "I saw the bodies of women and children lying in the doorways of their burning homes! That's butchery, the work of mad dogs—not soldiers!"

The filibuster's eyes were worried, but he shrugged his shoulders.

"That wasn't my men," he defended. "It was the Mexicans. They are mighty hard to hold in check. You know they have stood a lot from Toledaro, and now that their day is at hand they are likely to go to excesses—"

"Which you and Joab Burley—and the United States of America—will be blamed for," she reminded him; and Blankenship's furrowed brow revealed that her shot had registered.

The members of Blankenship's expedition, Diane noticed, were for the most part clean-cut American youths, eager to serve their country. Alarmed by the increasing number of Japanese in Mexico, they had been misled into believing that the preservation of America demanded the extreme measures they were taking. Poor, misguided youngsters who had been victimized by the dashing filibuster's glib tongue just as had Joab Burley!

But Diane realized the hopelessness of trying to argue with them, even when she could momentarily elude her watchful guards. The welcome Burley was receiving, and the expedition's triumphal progress through Chihuahua, seemed to bear out all of Blankenship's claims, whipping up the morale of his men to a fanatical frenzy. By the light in their eyes she could see that these poor dupes regarded themselves as modern crusaders….

Helplessly she stood by while that triumphal procession went on and the swelling expedition drove farther and farther into Mexico. Candelaria, Carrizal, Gallego, Torrazas and then the city of Chihuahua fell to the invaders. Onward they swept through village after village toward Santa Rosalia, which would give them domination of practically the whole of Mexico's largest state.

"With Chihuahua behind us, it will be a parade to Mexico City!" Sam Blankenship exulted—but before they reached Santa Rosalia there was the garrisoned town of Concho to be passed….

TOLEDARO'S FORCES had thrown up defenses outside the town, but they broke and fled in wild panic as soon as the charging Americans came at them with the cold steel that followed a preliminary barrage. Triumphantly, Blankenship led the way into the town and prepared to camp there for the night. Most of the buildings had been deserted, the populace evidently having fled with the routed federal troops, so Blankenship billeted his men in the empty buildings.

Jubilantly, the filibusters retired that night—but in the morning it was a stricken army that staggered out of the buildings of Concho, to stand blinking in the sun, covering their red-rimmed eyes with feeble, palsied hands. Weakly they staggered to the hospital tent, where the doctors examined them, and then sent a hurry call for Blankenship.

"These men are stricken with some sort of virulent tropical fever," the head doctor whispered his discovery. "What it is we can't say, but they are being wracked with dysentery and are running alarming temperatures. We have had more than fifty cases already—and the line seems endless. You know we haven't the medical equipment to cope with an epidemic."

Quickly Blankenship set out to investigate—and what he found appalled him. The fever seemed to have stricken one man out of every three, and already it was spreading alarmingly. The fear of death stared at him from the eyes of the sufferers— and panic was seizing their mates. Not until he noticed that no Mexican had come down with the fever did he realize that none of his Mexican allies had entered Concho; they had stayed outside and left the taking of the town entirely to the Americans. Even the few Mexican civilians who had remained, after Toledaro's troops had retired, seemed to have slipped away— until searching parties routed and carried them out of the holes where they had crept to die!

Wasted and gaunt, with eyes that burned in their skulls like balls of fire, they were in the last stages of the mysterious malady.

113

When questioned, they only shook their heads or mumbled that all the rest were dead—until the doctors won the gratitude of a withered oldster by relieving his pain.

"The sickness—it came a week ago," he quavered. "In two-three days everyone had it. They died—strong men and women and the little *ninos*. Concho became a town of death. We healthy ones tried to go away, but the soldiers would not let us. 'Contagion!' they said—so we had to stay until everyone was sick." His head drooped.

"The dead?" he answered a doctor's query. "The soldiers would not let us bury them. We had to put them in the cellars and on the house-tops—anywhere but in the ground. The soldiers were here to watch us. They wore masks so that they would not catch the plague, and they forced us to hide the bodies wherever we could find a place for them."

Concho was a pest-hole! Deliberately, diabolically, the town had been turned into a fiendishly conceived death-trap—and then surrendered to the invading Americans after only a pretended defense!

Seething with rage, Sam Blankenship set out to find the leaders of his Mexican allies. But when he reached the edge of town a cordon of machine guns, manned by gas-masked soldiers, greeted him. Concho was surrounded, every way of escape cut off.

"We can take no chances with this plague," one of the leaders who had pretended the greatest friendship for the Americans announced with a bald pretense of regret. "The town will have to be kept under quarantine until the disease is checked. There is nothing else that I can do—surely your doctors will agree to that."

Smooth words—with steel and bullets to back them up. Only then did Sam Blankenship realize that his "allies" had increased until they outnumbered his own force nearly ten to one! Well armed fighters who ringed the town with a wall that was impassable....

MEN DIED right and left during the next two days. Half a dozen times Blankenship attempted a desperate charge to break that imprisoning cordon. But always his overwhelmingly outnumbered men were thrown back into the pest-hole that promised to become their communal grave.

During those terrible days Diane Elliot was everywhere in the disease-ravaged town, braving the epidemic recklessly as she did her utmost to ease and aid the dying sufferers. Strangely the fever passed her by, just as it skipped Sam Blankenship, who was patrolling the limits of his terrible prison from daybreak until far into each night.

Finally, on the third day, he mustered every man who could stand on his feet and prepared for a last desperate charge. During the night he had discovered that the lines of his treacherous "allies" were weakest on the northern side of the town—and there he launched his attack. Frantically the Americans threw themselves against the gas-masked Mexicans. The imprisoning wall broke; the Mexicans fell back, and the stricken filibusters poured through the gap—headed north, toward the border.

Three times Sam Blankenship tried to swerve the route of that tragic flight, but always a solid wall of Mexican guns barred the way—kept him headed north. And at last he understood the full extent of the trap into which he had fallen. Those Mexican leaders who had greeted him and his men with open arms had been playing a treacherous part. They had been sent to him deliberately, to fool and lure him deep into Chihuahua. The excesses they had committed had been deliberate, to arouse all of Mexico against the United States and unite the country behind Toledaro.

Concho had been the last step in that fiendishly devised trap. Tricked into the death-ridden town, the Americans had been kept there until their entire force was stricken—and then they had been deliberately released, to be shepherded northward by their Mexican warders!

Shepherded back to the border with their fearful contamination....

Fully Sam Blankenship realized how he had been duped—but just as fully he realized his own helplessness. There was nothing to do but go on before death annihilated the remnants of his decimated force. As fast as they were able, they fled northward, leaving behind them their dead and those who were too ill to go any farther.

At Encinillas, Joab Burley was stricken, and swiftly his bulky frame wasted under the ravages of the disease. At Los Medanos, less than fifty miles from the border, he could go no farther. Death was reaching a grisly hand for him, and he knew it—but he clung to life tenaciously.

"So this is the end," he husked as Diane did her best to make his last moments more comfortable; "the end of it all. I have been

DIANE

a fool, Miss Elliot—a blind, conceited fool. I thought I saw a chance to go down in history as the man who added another row of stars to the American flag. Sonora, Chihuahua, Coahuila, Sinaloa, Durango, Nuevoleon, Tamaulipas, Zacatecas and San Luis Potosi," he slowly listed the names of the states which form the northern two-thirds of Mexico. "Those were the states

Joab Burley was going to bring into the Union—but that was a wild, impossible dream. Now history will record Joab Burley as a numbskull who was tricked and used as a dupe to lead his country into a disastrous and useless war." He shuddered.

"But I didn't know, Miss Elliot," he almost pleaded for understanding. "It wasn't for myself that I undertook this mad campaign. It was for America, to make our country stronger— the greatest and strongest in the world—because I wanted to see Old Glory waving triumphantly from the northernmost tip of Alaska to the Isthmus of Panamá! Believe me!"

With a last surge of strength, Joab Burley raised himself on one elbow as he was swept away by his own oratory, by one of those rhetorical flourishes that had been his stand-by all through life—and then suddenly the strength ebbed out of him and he was dead.

After Burley's death, Sam Blankenship was in complete command of the routed filibusters as they raced back to the United States—taking with them a raging death scourge that would be far worse than the might of the Japanese troops. A bitter, frustrated man, his dreams of empire shattered, his own short-comings pitilessly revealed to him, he ruled his men with an iron hand—and in the back of his bleak and inscrutable eyes a purpose began to take form and blaze with a terrible tensity....

CHAPTER 12
DEATH'S DWINDLING
NUMBERS

AFTER RODRIGUEZ had left to carry out More-los' orders to swing the army to the north, the revolution chieftain turned to Operator 5. For a moment he hesitated uncertainly, and Jimmy could see the indecision mirrored in his dark eyes. He owed much to this American who had snatched him from prison and probably had saved him from a firing squad. But finally the fiery patriotism that was typical of the man gained the mastery. His face set.

"And for you, *Americano*—" Morelos began, and then stopped short as the black snout of an automatic covered his belly.

"No, Avila," Jimmy Christopher said softly, as his weapon covered the grouped staff warily, "you do not have to place me under arrest. I shall save you that. I know nothing about this," he vowed earnestly, "but I cannot expect you to take my unsupported word for that. When I see you again it will be with proof that you cannot doubt. Until then—*adios, amigo!*"

Cautiously he backed his way to the door—and then he was gone into the night. Back to the northwest, over ground recently so hopefully won from Toledaro's men, he made his way, until he reached the town of Cervantes. There he located Jose Sanchez and sent out the call to bring in every available man.

Only six others answered that call—six men who were living on borrowed time, who rightfully should have met the same death they had seen strike down their companions.

"Someone betrayed us," Mark Crosby groaned. "The Japanese seemed to know just where to find us. I know of four who were seized and stood up against a wall to be shot. They almost caught Ed Weaver and me. But Ed managed to fight his way into a refinery, and he took at least two hundred Japs to hell with him when he blew it up over his head. Ed used to be my buddy in the old Ranger days back on the Arizona border."

"They almost trapped us, too." Tony Samaniego nodded gloomily. "But Fidel Castro tricked them neatly. He had a federal army captain's uniform, and in it he stole into the Japanese lines—told them that there was an unsuspecting force of Morelistas just ahead of them. Under his guidance they fell upon the enemy—one of Toledaro's crack regiments. Four or five hundred died before the mistake was discovered—but they hacked Fidel into little pieces with their heavy swords."

All through Mexico the members of that valiant little band were nobly living up to the oath they had sworn to Operator 5. Everywhere they were doing their utmost to cripple Toledaro and to hamper the Japanese. But their number was dwindling, melting away like a cake of ice exposed to the glare of the Mexican noonday sun—and now the invasion of America had actually begun.

"Burley and his pack of fools fell neatly into a trap," Richard Wilson reported when he arrived in Cervantes, looking like only a shadow of his stalwart self. "They were stricken with a malignant fever and died like flies on their way back to the border—and hot on their heels came the motorized columns of the Japanese. One column stormed El Paso, while another crossed the Rio Grande near Del Rio and has over-run all of southern and central Texas. The main column from El Paso is working up into New Mexico, to march into Colorado and seize the whole Western third of the United States. Nothing can stop them now, Operator 5—nothing short of a miracle!"

If nothing short of a miracle was required, then a miracle would have to be performed, Jimmy Christopher vowed grimly—and he set out to accomplish it. Disguised as Mexicans, he and his little band worked their way northward until they reached the Rio Grande and crossed it just south of Laredo. After that their slow progress was through a desolate land that plucked at their heart-strings.

Following in the wake of the Japanese, bands of marauding Mexicans were conducting a guerrilla warfare of their own—a warfare that consisted of plunder and pillage, of rape and atrocious murder. Like a swarm of devastating locusts, they swept over the land they had often eyed covetously from their own side of the Rio Grande—and behind them they left a trail of smoldering embers and mangled bodies.

"This isn't war—it's frightful barbarism, utter savagery unleashed!" Jimmy groaned, as they passed home after home that had been leveled to the ground; as they stopped to give burial to ghastly horrors that hardly could be recognized as the corpses of human beings!

A SCORE of times they held themselves sternly in check to avoid a clash with one of those harrying bands—a clash which could only result disastrously for their overwhelmingly outnumbered party. Individuals did not matter, Jimmy told himself again and again; it was the fate of America that was paramount. Much as they might want to stop and avenge those outrageous crimes—the path of duty lay straight ahead, where the spearhead of that Japanese drive was sinking deep into the vitals of America. Resolutely they closed their eyes and stopped their ears—until they approached a lonely ranch in the country west of the razed town of Fort Stockton. The smoke of its burning buildings had attracted them from afar, and when they came nearer they saw that a band of nearly a hundred Mexicans had surrounded the place. The outbuildings had already crumpled and were nothing more than collapsed bonfires. Now the raiders were ringing the low adobe ranch-house, pouring a steady hail of lead into it as they circled round and round on their horses.

Valiantly that garrison had withstood the assault of lead and fire, had even managed to extinguish the blaze when a wagonload of burning hay had been pushed up against the front door. But the guerrilla leader still had another trick up his sleeve. Behind the screen of a heavy farm truck, that had been pushed up within fifty feet of the building, his men were busily at work. Howls of evil anticipation rose from that wolf-pack when the truck was dragged away, and the devilment that had been going on behind it was exposed to the besieged defenders.

Lashed to the trunk of a sparsely branched live-oak was the naked body of a young woman, with a stack of wood and brush piled around her legs as high as her knees!

Jimmy Christopher caught one glimpse of her agonized face—and his heart leaped into his mouth. For a horrible moment he had been certain that the helpless captive was Diane Elliot!

Then he saw that he had been mistaken—but the near-recognition unnerved him, brought out a cold sweat all over his body. Diane... where was she now? He had had little time to think of her lately, but always in those last few moments, before he fell asleep, his thoughts had been with her.

But that poor girl tied to the tree—she was somebody else's Diane. Involuntarily, he crept closer through the cover of a prickly pear and dwarf-oak thicket, and behind him came Richard Wilson and the others. This must be no concern of theirs, warning whispered in his brain. He should be leading the way onward, losing not a moment on the way to El Paso... and yet he crept closer, closer.

Now he could see the girl's face, plainly. It was set in lines of despair, but her eyes were brave, her jaws firmly clenched.

"You have one more minute to open that door!" the guerrilla leader shouted to those behind the barricaded ranch-house windows—and instantly his voice was defiantly echoed.

"No, Paul—don't listen to him! Don't open that door or he will murder you all!" the girl pleaded. "I don't matter, darling—you must think of the babies!"

"Very well!" the chieftain mocked. Two men at his side knelt and fitted the shafts of blazing-pointed arrows to bows and shot them at the improvised stake.

In a few moments four of those arrows had found their mark and the brittle tinder was ablaze. Hungrily, the flames licked up around her naked body, laved her face and crowned her head with a fiery halo.

"Don't open, Paul! Don't open!" she shrieked in her fearful agony—and then a single shot came from the besieged building, the bullet plowing unerringly into her heart….

JIMMY CHRISTOPHER did not have to see those stout walls to know that her Paul had fired that shot—to see the man's convulsively working face, the tears that flooded his grim eyes and the sob that must have wrenched from his throat when her flame-seared face fell forward, her hair-denuded head limp on her blistered chest. Even in that moment of anguish, of heart-rending sympathy, a fierce pride surged through Operator 5. These were Americans! That fearless woman whose body was burning to a crisp, and the iron-willed husband and father who had courageously put an end to her agony—they were Americans, the sort of people who never could be conquered no matter how overwhelming the odds…. Heroically, that mother had died to save her loved ones—but at that moment Jimmy saw that her sacrifice had been in vain!

During the ghastly scene beneath the live-oak tree, others of the Mexicans had stolen up to the rear of the building and had gained the roof. A score of them were at work on it with axes, were setting a keg of powder in its center and lighting the fuse. Drawing back to the ends of the roof, they lay flat and waited for the blast. The moment it went off they were on their feet, swarming forward to leap down through the gaping hole onto the defenders below.

In a few moments the brief, desperate struggle in the building was over. Then the door was flung wide, and the captives were dragged out—haggard-eyed men, sobbing women—and three youngsters the oldest of whom could not have been six years old.

With a yelp of glee the guerrilla chieftain leaned forward to snatch up a curly-headed little girl who was whimpering and clinging timorously to her father's trouser leg—and in that moment the laughing fiend straightened in his saddle and then pitched to the ground with a bullet hole between his eyes. The iron will that was Operator 5's had been tried beyond endurance—and Jimmy Christopher's finger had pulled the trigger.

"Thank God for that!" Richard Wilson breathed fervently.

Suddenly the momentary stillness that had followed the leader's death was shredded by a blood-curdling Apache war-cry!

Leaping out of the thicket with guns blazing, Jimmy and the Indian led that onslaught. Behind them came seven others who seemed to be Mexicans but who poured a withering fire into the ranks of those astounded raiders. More than a score of the guerrilla band died before they had recovered from the shock of their leader's almost magical death—and then the rest came to their senses.

They outnumbered Jimmy's little band nearly ten to one, but they were matched against men whose marksmanship was perfect—men whose breasts were seething with horror and rage; men for whom death held no terrors. Darting to whatever cover they could find, those men, who had been holding themselves in check so long, finally had the opportunity for which they had been longing—and the vengeance they exacted was appalling. Mexicans died on every side. Raked by that deadly fire, and now

125

exposed to fresh volleys from the defenders who had run back to the windows of the ranch-house, their ranks were decimated. In a few minutes the blood-bathed ground was littered with corpses—and the handful of survivors of that murderous band were in panic-stricken retreat over the brush-dotted plain, with a last volley of shots speeding them on their way.

Stern-eyed, austere-lipped, Jimmy Christopher rose from where he had been lying prone on the ground behind the corpses of two of his victims. From the shelter of the farm truck, Jose Sanchez strode to join him, and then Richard Wilson came walking back disconsolately from his single-handed pursuit of the fleeing raiders—but they were all. Mark Crosby, Tony Samaniego and the others lay where they had fallen, mustered out of their country's service for all time.

With a heavy heart, Jimmy bade a silent farewell to those fallen comrades and left their bodies for the rescued ranch-men to bury, while he pressed on toward El Paso with Wilson and Sanchez. Constantly they crossed the desolated trail of marauding bands, and near Fort Hancock they encountered heavy parties of Mexicans, pressing northeast, which they could avoid only by re-fording the Rio Grande.

Finally they arrived in Juarez—only to find Mexican troops patrolling the river and permitting nobody to cross in either direction. El Paso, a shell-torn wreck of a city, had become a ghastly place of death. Cut off from the rest of the world, its only inhabitants were the survivors of the desperate defense against the Japanese onslaught—and they were dying on every side from the frightful ravages of a tropical fever that was raging unchecked among them!

CHAPTER 13
DEATH FROM ABOVE

A S GENERAL FERRARA watched Joab Burley's plane disappear into the south, he realized the full significance of the Triumvir's flight into Mexico—and realized, as well, his own inability to cope with the yellow tide that would now be unloosed upon the country. All that the Japanese needed was an excuse for their invasion, and now Burley was handing it to them.

Apologetically he turned to Tim Donovan, where he stood looking after the ship with bitter eyes that were already envisioning the collapse of all Operator 5's hopes.

"I'm sorry, Tim—I should have acted more quickly," he murmured. "But at first I could not grasp what you were telling me—it didn't seem possible that Joab Burley could be guilty of such treachery. I always considered him just a harmless poseur."

"The treachery angle probably never even occurred to him, General," Tim said shrewdly. "He is just being himself—just posing, admiring himself in the role of president of a new country, father of a new republic. But this time, he is playing into the hands of unscrupulous traitors who are using him as a cat's-paw. But we mustn't let them get away with it! We must stop them—somehow. If Operator 5 was here, I know what he would do—and I am going to do my best to do it in his stead!"

That indomitable spirit was infectious; Ferrara caught it and snapped out of the lethargy of indecision that had gripped him. Quickly he telegraphed to Andrew Warren and informed him what had happened—to start Warren rushing to El Paso. Then he pitched into the job of strengthening the border defenses, mustering every available man to stem the yellow flood that would come surging up from the south at any moment.

Meanwhile Tim Donovan had sent out an SOS to all of Jimmy Christopher's agents in the Southwest he could locate.

"Operator 5 is somewhere in Mexico," he told them, when a score of veteran undercover men responded to his call. "He is staking everything on his hope of stopping this Japanese invasion before it gets under way—but now his plans have been wrecked by Joab Burley's treacherous folly. The Japs will be rolling across the border any day, any hour—and we must be ready for them when they come!"

Those men turned to one another soberly and understood fully what was expected of them. Tried and trusted secret-service operatives, they had not been called upon to accompany Jimmy to Mexico because they were key-men, too important to be removed from the positions they occupied—and it was those positions that were now in peril.

During the past year Jimmy Christopher had been doing everything in his power to encourage the industrialization of the Southwest. He had made big strides in this rebuilding program. In this territory his influence had located many of the nation's most important munitions and armament plants—and those plants must not be allowed to fall into enemy hands! Each must be operated to capacity until the very last moment—then must be completely destroyed.

"They can be made to serve even as they are blown to atoms." A grizzled factory superintendent eyed his fellows. "Every building can be mined and wired so that it can be turned into a death-trap when the invaders take possession of it—but that may mean that the man who presses the final button will have no way of escape."

"We need a man like that responsible for each plant," another nodded agreement. "I will take care of the Abilene munition works."

"The Temple steel plant is already prepared," its representative announced. "The Japs will never have a chance to operate it."

"Count on me for the Phoenix powder mills," came another offer.

Prescott, Albuquerque, Wichita Falls, Waco, San Antonio— one by one the vital plants were designated to their pledged destroyers, until the map spread on the table in front of Tim Donovan was dotted with little circles, each representing an undercover man who had made his compact with death.

And those compacts were kept faithfully....

IN THE midst of Ferrara's frantic preparations, the storm broke. Hourly there had been rumors of Japanese troops in Chihuahua—and then a closed car drew up at the Juarez end of the International Bridge. Out of it staggered three emaciated wrecks of men who clutched useless rifles that they could hardly hold. For a moment they stood swaying drunkenly, trying to protect their eyes from the sun; then they seemed to grasp their surroundings. With delirious sobs on their lips they started across to El Paso in a lurching travesty of a run—and, as soon as they had reached the American side, after them came the first wave of the Japanese!

Determinedly, the waiting Americans hurled back that line, then huddled in their entrenchments while hell broke loose over the doomed city. Big guns pounded it, shells turned the streets into wreckage-piled canyons, planes rained death from overhead—and the Japanese engineers spanned the shallow river with a dozen pontoon bridges over which their tanks and armored trucks poured. Wave after wave of the well armed and completely mechanized troops swept up to the defending entrenchments—until those ramparts no longer existed.

Over the corpse-cluttered ditches the Japs swarmed, into the shell-shattered, blazing town beyond; while the Americans fell back, fighting doggedly each foot of the way.

El Paso was lost, but it was no longer a city—it was no more than a shambles, Sylvester Ferrara saw, as he strove to hold his men in line, to stiffen the resistance and reform the defense miles to the north. The Japs had taken the city, but they had paid heavily for their victory, thanks to the advance information that had come from Operator 5.

Acting on that information, Ferrara had concentrated his troops where they could do the maximum of damage. At El Paso and in Southern Texas they were waiting—waiting to yield their lives before the invaders passed. And behind them were those others who waited just as grimly.

One by one, those circles on Tim Donovan's map were blotted

out by crosses—crosses that marked the graves of men who had kept their pledges, and of thousands of Japanese invaders who had died with them. One by one, the industrial plants Operator 5 had striven so indefatigably to establish were blown into bits, and slowly the desperately fighting American line was pushed backward until most of Texas was lost and the yellow horde was beginning to over-run New Mexico and Arizona.

Fifty miles north of El Paso, General Ferrara tried to make a stand. Feverishly the wearied fighters dug in and tried to erect entrenchments that would have some chance of withstanding the merciless onslaught shortly to batter against them. Worriedly Ferrara stood outside his headquarters on the edge of Roswell and conferred with Andrew Warren.

"Man for man we can stand against them, even though they have superior rifles and machine-guns, not to mention that almost bullet-proof armor they wear. But it is the tanks—tanks and planes—that take the heart out of our resistance," he said. "Human flesh simply will not stand up against steel, no matter how firm the will behind it. Here they come again!" His eyes turned skyward.

As he spoke, nearly fifty of the scarlet Japanese planes came soaring northward. When they were behind the American lines they circled lower—and out from beneath them plummeted dark figures that checked their precipitate downfall when parachutes blossomed out above them.

"Machine-gunners—our men will be caught front and rear!" Andrew Warren groaned, as he visualized a repetition of the tactics that had twice decimated the American forces just when they seemed to be making a successful stand. "If only we had adequate anti-aircraft protection!" One of the down-coming figures landed almost directly in front of them, and Ferrara raced forward, gun in hand, to meet the deadly blast of lead he expected at any moment. But the arrival from the sky lay limp and unmoving. Warily Warren and Ferrara bent over the still figure, gazed down into the face of a corpse—gazed into the hollow-eyed, cadaverous-cheeked face of Joab Burley!

"Joab!" Warren gasped. "How—"

"Pestilence!" Ferrara grasped the situation immediately. "God only knows what he died of—but look at that mottled skin. His whole body is burned out with consuming fever, and he was dumped here to spread the plague in our ranks!" Running to his horse, he raced up and down the line. His worst fears were promptly realized. For a length of miles the bodies of dead and dying victims of the plague were raining down behind the American lines. Sam Blankenship's men were returning to their native soil—and bringing with them the virulent seeds of death!

Already the defending troops were gathering around these amazing arrivals, staring down in awe at the disease-wracked corpses and doing the best they could do assuage the misery of those who still clung to life.

"Away from them!" Ferrara barked. "Leave them where they have fallen. You men who have touched them go to a first-aid station immediately for a thorough disinfectant. Those men mean certain death—not only for you but for all America! The whole line moves back." He issued crisp orders. "We will take up a new position five miles to the north—and leave these corpses here to greet the Japs when they come forward."

"But some of them aren't corpses, sir," one of his officers objected uncertainly. "Some of them are still alive. We can't just leave them lying here to die in agony—"

"No—" Sylvester Ferrara's voice was low, his face grim, as he nodded in acknowledgment of the report of a physician who had just examined one of the dying men—"we can't leave them here to die in agony. But there is no hope of saving them. The most humane thing we can do for them is to put an end to their misery—with a mercy bullet…."

All along the line grim-faced men stood over those groaning victims and triggered guns close to their temples. Bleak-faced men who gulped and found the will to carry out their role of executioner only when they read the mute appeal and thanks in the eyes of the doomed ones who asked nothing more than to be put out of misery.

THAT GRISLY task had no more than been finished when there was a diversion in the Japanese lines that set every American defender on the alert, at his post with finger ready on his rifle trigger. The enemy line was opening, was drawing back to allow a tattered procession to file through it and stagger across the No-Man's-Land that separated them from the Americans. A lean, hollow-eyed, half-naked band who looked as if they were stumbling back out of the jaws of hell.

General Ferrara stared at the approaching scarecrows through his field-glasses and snapped quick orders to concentrate a score of machine-guns on them.

"The last of Joab Burley's filibusters," he identified as he studied them. "But they are rotten with disease. We have no choice, Andrew. If we allow them to reach our lines, they will spread disease that will wipe out our army and spread from one end of America to the other. Our only hope is to dispatch them—and pray that that will check the spread of the scourge before it gets out of control."

Andrew Warren groaned and shook his head in helpless agreement. Grimly Ferrara steeled himself to give the order to fire—when suddenly Tim Donovan grasped his arm and whirled him around.

"That's Diane—Diane Elliot!" he shouted wildly, as he recognized a tattered, half-naked figure in the front rank of the doomed column.

Diane could hardly walk. She staggered along and was kept from falling only by the arm of Sam Blankenship. A gaunt scarecrow of a man, his husky frame emaciated until it was hardly recognizable, he led the surviving members of his ill-fated expedition in that march of death.

"It doesn't matter," Ferrara groaned. "She is like the rest—"

But Blankenship had turned and shouted an order to his tatterdemalion followers. They halted, stood swaying, holding one another up, while he cupped his hands and shouted toward the American lines.

"We are coming no closer," he announced hoarsely. "We're doomed; we know that. But we've done enough harm. We are going out onto the desert to die—out into the wilderness where nobody else will contract our curse. But—" his voice rose louder, rang with the old note of command—"this girl stays here to receive medical attention! You can't turn her away—"

"She is infected like the rest," Ferrara repeated almost to himself. "We can make no exceptions, not even for Operator 5!"

He hesitated, mustering his courage to give the fatal command to fire—but at that moment Tim Donovan and a companion snatched the decision out of his hands. Leaping from behind the hastily improvised defense barrier, they suddenly charged forward and did not stop until they were at Blankenship's side.

For a moment the blazing-eyed filibuster held Diane's almost limp body close. Then he relinquished her, and she was being carried back to the American lines—while he whirled to rivet his fiery glance on the doomed column. Silently, hopelessly, they turned at right-angles and shuffled off to the west, to the arid desert that would be their sepulcher....

CHAPTER 14
DEATH FROM BELOW

NORTH AND northwest from the ruins of El Paso spread the Japanese hordes. Back, steadily back, their irresistible motorized battering-ram smashed its way; up into New Mexico, and westward into Arizona and toward the rich goal of the California coast. General Isogai marked the advance on his maps.

The end was near.

Desperately the Americans tried to cling to the mining town of Bisbee, poured a deadly fire down from the steep hills that surround it. But the Japanese flying fortresses bombed and machine-gunned them from their positions—drove them back in an utter rout that amounted to annihilation of that part of the line. Triumphantly the yellow men pushed on into Arizona, their advance patrols forging miles ahead of the main column.

It was on the edge of old Tombstone—that roaring mining town which had made frontier history when the West was young—that one of those advance patrols came upon an old prospector who stumbled along the road like a sleep-walker. His face was thin and bearded, his eyes wild and staring, his clothing worn and dirt-caked—but his pockets bulged suspiciously.

"Halt! Where you go?" the spokesman for the patrol demanded, but the old man seemed not to hear him; seemed not even to see him.

As he came closer, the Japs could see that his lips were moving, that he was talking softly to himself—gesturing and laughing silently at his own conversation. Curiously they watched him, half-inclined to shoot him and end the matter. Then one of them noticed that a pocket of the old fellow's tattered trousers had given way and was trailing something in a fine shower out onto the road.

Something that glinted in the sunlight!

Quickly he stooped, examined it—and saw that the grain-like particles were yellow and gleamed dully. Coarse, heavy grains of what must be—*gold!*

In a moment the soldiers were all around the desert rat, were pinning his arms behind his back while they emptied out his pockets. They produced more than two heaping handsful of the yellow metal in dust and heavy nuggets that held their eyes like magnets.

"What this?" the English-speaker demanded. "Where you get?"

"Gold! Gold!" the oldster quavered. "I allus said there was gold in Tombstone. The fools said that when the silver run out the town was dead as its name—but I knowed better. I allus said there was gold—an' now I c'n prove it! That's gold—pure gold! I know where there's lots more of it—bonanza gold, I tell yer!"

Vacantly they stared at him, understanding only one word in every dozen he spoke—but one word they did understand was "gold." Their eyes sparkled. Avarice flashed in them, as they regarded one another and mutely suggested the possibility of forcing this old fellow to take them to his mine so that they could loot it for themselves. But at that moment another patrol came along the road—and its leader, a Captain Hiruse, took immediate charge.

"He must be taken back to headquarters," he ruled. "General Isogai will want to know of this immediately."

GENERAL ISOGAI did want to know of that immediately. The moment the dust and nuggets were dumped out onto the table that served him as a desk his dark, murky brown eyes narrowed to excited pinpoints. But his reaction was nothing compared to that of the Mexican officers attached to his staff. They ran their fingers through the coarse metal lovingly, and their faces were wreathed in smiles that strove valiantly to conceal the cupidity that gleamed in the depths of their eyes.

"They all thought old Ben Nolan was a fool." The old fellow

SAIGONI

SAM BLANKENSHIP

TOLEDARO

JOAB BURLEY

138

THE DAY OF THE DAMNED

MORELOS

TIM DONOVAN

DR. NORMAN KING

ANDY BRETTON

grinned fatuously when they plied him with smoothly worded questions. "Thought I didn't know nothin'—but I showed 'em. Right in the middle o' Tombstone—right in the Million Dollar Stope that they said was worked out—I found gold that's worth more than all the silver they ever took out of it. Heh, heh, old fool, am I? Well, mebbe now we'll see!"

"The Million Dollar Stope—that is right in the center of Tombstone, the next town to the northwest," one of the Mexicans babbled excitedly. Then he tried to cram the words back into his throat when he saw that Isogai was nodding and smiling with satisfaction.

"We shall go there," the commander announced. "I shall see this place where gold can be picked up by the handful. This assistance we are giving your country is expensive, Colonel Guaralara—Japan can use some of the yellow metal to help defray the bills."

Isogai's hand was on the butt of his automatic, and his subordinates were reaching for their weapons. Colonel Guaralara's upper lip curled back over his teeth and his eyes blazed with sudden undisguised hate. In that moment his intense dislike for these yellow allies, with whom he must cooperate, flared openly—then it was veiled behind a set mask of a smile.

The crisis that had threatened to set the Japanese and Mexicans at one another's throats was past, but each had read plainly in the eyes of the other the real feeling that existed between them. And now each would watch the other like a hawk....

"By all means, we shall go there," Colonel Guaralara bowed.

"We Mexicans are more familiar with this country than is the general, and we shall be glad to escort him."

Ben Nolan rode back to Tombstone in style—on the front seat of the first of five automobiles loaded down with Japanese and Mexican officers. The old mining town, deserted after its heyday at the turn of the century, had revived as a small Western residential town and tourist resort until the soldiers of the Purple Empire had overrun it and wantonly destroyed most of its old buildings. Some of them still remained, however, and the Japanese gazed at them curiously as Nolan led the way down the main street—past an old saloon that had once rung with the lusty voices and thundering six-guns of hardy miners and Western bad-men—to the great hole in the ground that was the Million Dollar Stope.

"Gold! Gold!" he chortled. "The fools said the silver was gone—an' they never found the gold. Not till old Ben Nolan come a-lookin'!"

Close on his heels they followed the apparently sun-touched old-timer down the shaley slide that was the mouth of the stope and then into the long-abandoned galleries. Farther and farther into the dusty, rock-strewn workings, the Japanese adding the beams of their flashlights to the torch Nolan had lighted and was holding overhead.

"Gold! Gold!" Ben Nolan chuckled. "They want a belly full of gold— let the dirty rats have it, boys!"

Whirling suddenly, he dashed his torch straight into the faces of the close-pressing officers—and before they could grab him, before they could beat him over the head with their pistols, the

141

center of the earth seemed to rend itself apart with a terrific detonation! One ear-shattering blast after the other—and then the old galleries were crumbling, the walls buckling, the ceilings coming down!

Wild, exultant yells—howls that seemed to come from the very pit of hell—rang through those long-abandoned workings as the Million Dollar Stope collapsed and settled tons of rock and dirt on the pulped bodies of General Isogai and all his staff... and also on the last fever-stricken survivors of the expedition that was to have made Sam Blankenship the dictator over all America.

Rather than spread disease throughout the nation, the filibusters had done their best to atone for their blind folly. Working with Ben Nolan, who had been deemed too old to go down into Mexico with Operator 5, they had buried themselves alive with the directing brains of the invaders!

More than a score of officers perished in those workings far beneath the street level of Tombstone. Hundreds of Japanese soldiers, who had been crowding close to the mouth of the stope, were also plunged into it when the ground gave way beneath them—were blown to pieces before they could extricate themselves. Wild confusion followed that catastrophe. Japanese and Mexicans were running everywhere; wounded survivors were climbing out of the huge grave that had almost engulfed them—and in the excitement nobody noticed a tall, gaunt, smoke-blackened figure who crawled out of the wreckage and unobtrusively wormed his way to the rear of the invaders' lines....

TENACIOUSLY SYLVESTER FERRARA clung to every foot of ground. But, once he was forced to retreat behind the disease-infested corpses the invaders rained from the sky, the Japanese drove him back relentlessly. Protected by gas masks, they had no fear of those plague-breeding remains. Over the bodies they charged, to drive the retreating Americans back far beyond the five miles Ferrara had intended to yield.

Back, back—swiftly the whole state of New Mexico was being wrested from him, until at last he made a desperate stand a few miles south of Santa Fe. Now the Japanese must be stopped or they would swarm up into Colorado and overrun the whole West.

Feverishly the harried but grimly determined troops were working to complete a last defense behind this line, in the city of Santa Fe itself. On the grounds of the old post office a fortress was rising—a two-story quadrangle on the style of the famous Texas Alamo, except that the thick walls of this structure were made of concrete and reënforced with facings of sheet iron and steel.

"Beyond that the invaders *cannot* go," Sylvester Ferrara vowed as he faced Andrew Warren. "If they do, there will be no more America. Once they spread over the West and reach the Mississippi, the fate of the Eastern states will be sealed. At Santa Fe they *must* be stopped—if we have to erect an insurmountable wall of corpses to block the way. But first we must hold this line as long as we possibly can. Every hour means more time to strengthen the fortress—"

As he spoke, he had been peering through his field-glasses;

now they came down from his eyes and amazement stopped his voice. Out there in the body-strewn, shell-torn wilderness that was No Man's Land, he had seen what appeared to be a tattered Mexican stagger up to an outpost and be dragged into the safety of a barricade as spiteful bullets whined after him in a sudden shower. A few moments later, the human scarecrow appeared again, coming back from the line, and now Ferrara recognized the nondescript figure as Operator 5!

"Thank God, Jimmy!" Andrew Warren raced to meet him, tears running down his cheeks. "We thought you had perished down there somewhere. But you are back—and now I *know* that the tide will turn!"

"I managed to slip across to El Paso at night," Jimmy quickly answered their questions. "Somehow I got through that terrible place without contracting the plague, and I have been in hiding ever since, working my way slowly northward until I had a chance to make a dash for your line. You haven't much more time, General. They are rushing up reinforcements and getting all set for another assault—"

His words were drowned out by a whoop of wild joy, and Tim Donovan came racing forward, to clasp his hand and throw an arm around his shoulder. Tim's freckled face was beaming with delight—but suddenly the happiness faded from it and he became mute, tongue-tied.

"What is it, Tim?" Jimmy Christopher pressed. "There is something vitally wrong, I can see that—something you don't want me to know. What is it?" And then he divined the answer.

"It's Diane," he said quickly. "What has happened to her, Tim? Tell me frankly."

Tim Donovan gulped, and it seemed that words would not come.

"Diane," he muttered miserably. "She has it, Jimmy—the tropical fever. Blankenship brought her back from Mexico more dead than alive, and since then she has been getting worse...."

His voice trailed off into silence, but Jimmy seized him by the shoulders and looked straight in the eyes. "How bad is she— man to man?" he demanded.

"The doctors have been doing their best, but she's bad, Jimmy." Tim's eyes misted. "They—they gave her chances up this morning. It may be—all over by now."

"Where is she?" the question lashed.

"In the general hospital in Santa Fe."

WITHOUT WAITING to hear any more, Jimmy Christopher had whirled and was racing to where several horses were tethered outside the hut that served as American staff headquarters. Leaping into one of the saddles, he spurred the animal to top speed and galloped off to Santa Fe—urged the horse on ceaselessly until he galloped up in front of the hospital and flung himself to the ground, to sprint up the stone steps into the soldier-crowded building.

"Diane Elliot—she is Doctor King's private patient," a nurse told him, and led him to the little bedroom where Norman King sat beside a white cot on which Diane lay so still and pale that she seemed to be....

Icy fingers clamped around Jimmy's heart, and he refused

even to think the ghastly thought that was rushing into his mind. Wide-eyed and open-mouthed, he stood there in the doorway. Then Norman King saw him; saw him and raised a warning hand for silence.

"She is all right," he whispered, and struggled to keep the exultation out of his voice. "She has passed the crisis, and now she will live. All she needs is sleep and rest."

For a moment Jimmy Christopher stood beside the cot and looked down at that still face, and his lips moved in a voiceless prayer of thanksgiving. Throat-choked, he turned away and followed the tired-looking doctor out into the corridor. "I've won, Operator 5!" Norman King said, as he softly closed the sick-room door. "I knew that there must be some place for a physician to be of real service. Toledaro's agents almost put me out of the running in New York, but I was being saved for better things—for this crisis the plague would bring down here."

He went on. "Tim and I carried Miss Elliot back into the lines, when Blankenship brought her over the border, and I have been quarantined with her here ever since. I've worked night and day—but at last I have isolated the fever germ and found an antidote for it. I've licked the scourge, man. I can cure the victims now unless the fever gets too much of a head-start!"

"You have isolated the germ—and you can cure the victims." Jimmy Christopher repeated the words slowly; and as he did a wild, daring plan leaped into his mind—a desperate inspiration that might prove to be the salvation of America!

Swiftly he outlined it to Dr. King. As he spoke, the physician nodded his head in quick understanding; then set to work packing his medicine bag to answer the most momentous call a man of medicine ever faced.

That night an unlighted plane darted through the network of searchlight beams that sought it and sped Operator 5 and Dr. Norman King, America's last tenuous hope, over the Japanese-Mexican lines....

CHAPTER 15
FREEDOM IN THE BALANCE

WITH THE catastrophic death of General Isogai and his entire staff, the Japanese drive was momentarily threatened with demoralization—but then Prince Saigoni sprang into the breach and took personal command of the invading troops. Relentlessly he pushed forward with a savagery that far exceeded Isogai's ruthless military tactics.

Smiling with satisfaction, he sat at a table in his headquarters, a safe distance behind the lines that were sweeping on toward Santa Fe, and gloated over the field map spread before him—a map that was gradually being shaded with red as the crimson tide of Orientals swept over it.

"Tomorrow we take Santa Fe," he chuckled, "and that will be the end of American resistance. After that we will divide our forces. I will lead the advance into Colorado and on to the Mississippi—and who can say how much farther it may be necessary for us to go? The Mexicans we will allow the pleasure of crossing the deserts into California and reclaiming the West Coast states their friends the gringos took away from them. One quick, paralyzing drive that carries everything before it—that will leave the United States prostrate, on its knees before any other effort at effective resistance can be attempted."

Complacently he traced the course of his contemplated triumphal march, and the dark eyes in his suave face gleamed with anticipation.

"Good night, gentlemen," he dismissed the members of his staff. "Sleep well—tomorrow morning we arise early, to resume our travels!"

But before he could retire to his own quarters an orderly appeared at his door to announce the arrival of two messengers from Avila Morelos.

"Messengers from Avila Morelos," Saigoni repeated, and his bland smile widened as he faced the orderly. "No doubt to report further successes against the Americans. Show them in, Tasu—show them in. We must encourage Brother Morelos to continue his good work—until we are ready to crush him for the rebellious dog that he is. Show them in."

Tasu had no opportunity to show in the messengers. Before he could turn to back out of the door, an automatic crashed down on his skull and he dropped like a poled steer. Over his falling body leaped one of the Mexicans who had downed him— and the automatic muzzle was jammed against Prince Saigoni's convulsing throat.

"One yelp out of you, and I pull the trigger!" a tense voice rasped in his ear, and the muzzle jabbed deeper to emphasize the warning.

Before Saigoni could regain control of his trembling lips,

the other Mexican had him by the wrist, was twisting his arm upward, to pull back his sleeve and jab the needle of a hypodermic syringe deep into his flesh. Saigoni's eyes widened. Then they filled with stark fear, as he watched the brownish contents of that glass barrel diminish when the evil-looking concoction squirted into his veins.

"Yes, Saigoni—" Jimmy Christopher nodded—"that dose is just as bad as it looks. It is a culture that is alive with plague virus—the same hellish plague you turned loose on Joab Burley's expedition. You have enough of it in you to kill off an army!"

The Eurasian's olive-hued skin blanched, became a sickly yellow-green, and wild panic leaped in his quailing eyes.

"You are trying to bluff—you think you can scare me!" he panted.

"Have you watched any of those plague victims die, Saigoni?"

"I will have your eyes burned out! The flesh will be stripped back from your fingers, from your hands and arms—"

"And that will not help you the slightest bit." Jimmy's voice was calm and unimpressed. "There is only one hope for you, Saigoni—and that lies with this gentleman, Dr. King. He has isolated the fever germ and knows the antidote for it. He is the only man in the world who can save your miserable life."

Saigoni's face worked spasmodically. His eyes threatened to pop out of his head, and saliva drooled unheeded down his jowls. For a moment he tried to speak, tried to continue his bluster— and then he capitulated abjectly. Suddenly his nerve snapped. The last bit of fear-spawned defiance ebbed from him, and he dropped to his knees, clawed frantically for Norman King's hand as he begged for reprieve from the death he had inflicted upon thousands of innocent victims.

"I will do anything—anything you say, Doctor!" he promised frantically. "I will make you the most powerful man in all America—the richest man on the American continents. Anything, Doctor, anything—but hurry, before it is too late! The antidote—"

"There is just one thing you can do, Saigoni." Jimmy eyed him remorselessly. "You will do it before Doctor King administers the antidote that will save your life. You will go with us to Avila Morelos' headquarters, and there you will confess every bit of your trickery and treachery. I know the truth, all of it—and the moment you try to lie you will be left there to die as you have brought death to so many others."

"Who are you—you devil?" Saigoni gasped.

"The man you thought you killed in Mexico City—Operator 5," Jimmy told him—and the Eurasian's last semblance of composure fled.

"I'll do anything—anything you say!" he babbled hysterically. "Only hurry! Hurry or it may be too late!"

"The speed depends upon you, Saigoni," Jimmy told him. "Call your chauffeur and order him to get your car—and remember, if you try to double-cross us, you doom yourself!"

Saigoni understood that perfectly, and he obeyed to the letter. Quickly he summoned his chauffeur and issued curt orders— heaped blasphemy on the man when he dared to question. A few minutes later the car was ready, and then it was speeding through the night in a wild dash for the headquarters from which Morelos was directing the invasion of Texas....

THAT TRIP took hours, and Saigoni died a thousand deaths on the way. It was almost dawn before the racing car roared up to the half-wrecked hotel where Morelos had quartered his staff; and ten minutes later before the revolutionist chieftain could be gotten from his bed to listen to Saigoni's babbled confession.

"Oh, so it is Operator 5!" His eyebrows arched questioningly when he recognized his callers. "Operator 5—with Prince Saigoni?"

"I promised you a visit, Morelos," Jimmy reminded him; "a visit with proof of the trickery that has been worked upon you. Here I am. You can talk now, Saigoni."

Saigoni wet his lips and regarded the heavily armed Mexican chieftain nervously, but his terror prodded him on.

"It is as he says," he confessed. "Burley's invasion of Mexico was my doing. My men played with him, tricked the silly fool into believing that the northern states of Mexico were waiting to be liberated. He thought he would be hailed as an emancipator and that he would be able to annex all the northern states to the American Union. I instigated that invasion so that there would be an excuse for pursuing the invaders across the border and then overrunning the United States."

"And Blankenship?" Jimmy prompted.

"Blankenship—I tricked him, also," Saigoni admitted. "I promised to set him up as dictator of all Mexico and the Western half of the United States, if he would lead the invasion. He thought that the anti-Toledaro forces in Mexico would join him and that my Japanese would rise and overthrow the president at the last moment. I had to enlist him because Burley never could have organized the invading army. Blankenship was to organize the men, while Burley lent his name to the expedition and involved the United States so that our own invasion would be justified…. That is all," he turned to King. "I have told everything—now you will do your part. Now the cure—before it is too late!"

"Not yet," Jimmy Christopher ruled firmly. "First, I want Señor Morelos to hear how neatly you tricked Toledaro."

"He is a fool!" Saigoni fairly screamed. "He sees nothing but a chance to enrich himself at the expense of the Americans. He thinks that he will get back the states that Mexico lost a hundred years ago—but he does not see that he has become a helpless puppet. Within a few months, we will have half a million Japanese soldiers here and Mexico will become a Japanese protectorate. I have only used him so that Japan would have an excuse to invade the United States without declaring a war that might meet the condemnation of the rest of the world…. Now, surely, I have told everything!" he pleaded. "Now you will no longer withhold the cure. Your bargain, Operator 5—"

"That seems to cover about everything," Jimmy nodded; "except that you might tell Señor Morelos what we overheard when we entered your quarters a few hours ago. I think he will be interested to know that you regard him as a rebellious dog and intend to crush him as soon as you are finished using him and his men."

As Avila Morelos listened, his dark eyes became bleak.

Nervously his fingers closed on the haft of a knife that was sheathed at his belt, but Jimmy Christopher's steady gaze held him in check. Now his eyes blazed with deadly hatred, and Saigoni backed away from him fearfully—cowered behind King as the doctor administered the promised injection.

"I should have known," Morelos muttered. "I, too, have been a blind fool—no more than clay in the cunning hands of this perfidious devil. But it is not too late to give him his proper reward. My men will withdraw from this invasion immediately, Operator 5—and we will march back into Mexico. Back to Mexico City to overthrow the traitor Toledaro and expel these Japanese invaders! You, Saigoni, are under arrest. You will be held until I capture Toledaro, and then you will both be tried for treason—executed together! Manuel—Juan!" he shouted; and a moment later the poisonous Eurasian was being led away by two of Morelos' guards.

Halfway to the doorway they got with their prisoner—when suddenly the door was flung open and a wild man stood glaring at them. A blackened scarecrow whose tattered rags of clothing hung from the gaunt skeleton of what had once been a magnificent body.

Saigoni stared.

"Blankenship!" he gasped recognition and then tried desperately to back away.

But Sam Blankenship leaped forward with a bound that was astounding in a man so weakened. Out of his rags flashed a knife that whipped up and plunged deep into Saigoni's throat. Again and again it rose and descended.

At last the guards came to their senses. One of them clubbed his rifle and swung it at the filibuster's head—but Blankenship went down even before the heavy butt crashed against his skull. The last ounce of strength had drained from his wasted body as he settled the score with the man who had betrayed him....

Blood was gushing from half a dozen fatal wounds as Prince Saigoni sank to the floor, and the knowledge of certain death was in his eyes. Curiously, it seemed to release him from the abject cowardice that had shackled him and had reduced him to a whimpering spectacle. Now he raised himself on one elbow and glared vindictively at Jimmy Christopher.

"You think you have won, American, but your victory will turn to ashes in your mouth," he taunted maliciously. "I will not live to witness the triumph, but your men in Santa Fe are doomed. My troops have surrounded your makeshift fortress and will break into it at any moment now. For days the poor fools have been laboring building a trap—while we watched and laughed at them."

Weakly he pointed to the rising sun.

"At dawn this morning the order will be given to close in from three sides. In an hour's time Santa Fe will be a heap of crumbling ruins and its survivors will be penned up in their trap, waiting for the sure death that will come to every one of them. Your Triumvirs, Ferrara and Warren, will die there, Operator 5—and the gateway will be open—to all the Western half—of your leaderless country. See that sun—the invincible red sun of Japan! It is rising—"

With a final taunt on his lips, Prince Saigoni, who was to

have been the Regent of America, joined the company of his mixed ancestors.

Operator 5 stared down at the immobile features that once more were suave and inscrutable in death, but his grim eyes were seeing far beyond the Eurasian's faintly mocking face; were seeing into that beleaguered fortress where Andrew Warren and Sylvester Ferrara—and probably Diane Elliot—were waiting for certain death....

CHAPTER 16
THE SECOND ALAMO

DAWN HAD barely grayed the sky when hell broke loose outside Santa Fe. With the first beams of the rising sun, the Japanese went into action. The ground-shaking thunder of their big guns heralded the attack and fairly pulverized the inadequate barricades behind which the American defenders crouched. A barrage that leveled the entrenchments and pitted the terrain with gaping shell-holes—and on top of that came the rumbling charge of the tanks and the heavily armored "fire wagons" from which streams of liquid flame bathed the ground and crisped everything within reach.

Thousands of the defenders fell beneath that withering onslaught and were ground into the earth under the steel treads of the tanks and the heavy boots of the Japanese infantry. The dazed, battered survivors staggered back to their second line—which had crumpled beneath the terrible pounding even before they reached it. Utterly routed, and fleeing helplessly before the merciless death that followed them, they straggled into Santa Fe only to find that the city was being blown to pieces around them.

Buildings were toppling and crashing on every side. Streets were piled with debris and littered with the bodies of non-combatants who had been cut down in the midst of frantic flight. From three sides the Japanese were pounding the town, until scarcely a building remained standing—scarcely a building but the fortress in its very center.

Into that haven the terrified women and children were streaming, and toward it the grimly battling men converged. Now the waves of Japanese troops were closing in inexorably from the same three sides, following in the wake of the big guns' destruction with a devastating hail of machine-gun lead that melted all resistance before it. Desperately the harried Americans contested every foot of the way—but they could do no more than die and over their corpses swept the Japanese horde.

Back, back—until they were under the shell-scarred walls of the newly built fortress; until they were penned up within its four sides and the Japanese flood swirled up and surrounded it.

"The second Alamo," Sylvester Ferrara had dubbed the fort when it was being built; but he had not realized the fatal aptness of the name until he found himself and his men trapped within the shell-battered walls.

Nearly three thousand Americans, the remnants of the defending troops and the women and children from the city, herded into that refuge before the heavy doors were closed and barred—but within an hour their number had been reduced by almost half. Now that the city was demolished, the big guns

156

had moved in closer and every muzzle was trained on the little quadrangle that was the last obstacle to bar the yellow men from all of America.

High-powered shells hailed against it, and the terrific explosions tore great gaping holes through steel and concrete. No fortification could stand such a pounding for long, and this one had been rushed to completion with inadequate materials. Gradually, it began to go to pieces. Now it would be but a matter of time before a section of it would be leveled—then wave after wave of armored Japanese would come pouring through the aperture, and that would be the end….

TRIUMVIR ANDREW WARREN was everywhere in that beleaguered deathtrap. From side to side he went, encouraging the desperate defenders, heartening them by his own indifference to danger. Helping to man one of the few defending field-pieces, when most of its crew was killed; springing behind a machine-gun when its gunner fell dead over its hot barrel; grasping a rifle and taking his place at one of the gun-ports when the yellow tide threatened to sweep over the wall; touring through the hospital wards where a score of women were doing their best to save the lives of the terribly wounded fighters who were being carried back from the walls in a steady stream. The Triumvir seemed to be in a dozen places at once.

"Jimmy will come back with help," he stopped to reassure Diane Elliot, where she was tossing restlessly on a cot, kept there only by Dr. King's warning that she would be tied down if she tried to get up.

But the moment his back was turned the reassuring smile

vanished from his face and doubt clutched at his heart. Worriedly he went back to the front wall, which was taking the worst battering and threatened to be the section that would give way. Sylvester Ferrara was in charge there; was doubling the defenders at the half-wrecked ports in a desperate effort to stop the onslaught that would come at any moment.

"Five minutes more at the most," he turned a grim, set face to his fellow-Triumvir. "This wall can't possibly hold out longer than that."

Out over the wrecked city, he turned his gaze—out over ruins that were pitted with machine-gun nests, battle-torn streets that were dotted with the corpses of Japanese infantrymen who looked like fantastic creatures from another world in the light, modernized version of their ancient, scale-like armor. Thousands and thousands of them crouched there just waiting for the command to sweep forward....

"The name of Operator 5 has become almost a magic talisman," he said softly, as if he were talking to himself rather than to Warren. "We have come to expect miracles from him—but this is too much to ask. I have been hoping against hope that he would find some way to come to our rescue, but no man can help us now. This is the end, Andrew. I have seen Jimmy Christopher work his last miracle—"

A terrific explosion drowned out his words, and a whole section of the wall seemed to disintegrate. Steel and concrete flew in every direction and for a moment the whole world seemed to become a blinding cloud of flame and smoke and choking dust.

Andrew Warren was flung backward, was hurled across the room by that blast. Stunned and bleeding from cuts on his head and face, he staggered to his feet and turned to find death all around him. In front of him a great hole had been blown in the wall, and in the piles of wreckage behind it lay the torn bodies of the defenders who had been half-buried.

More than a score of them—and among them lay Sylvester Ferrara!

Still half-stunned by the shock, Warren groped his way to the fallen general, tried to lift some of the shattered concrete that pinned him down—until he saw that Ferrara's chest was crushed completely.

With a roar like that of an avalanche another section of the weakened wall crumpled into shattered rubble—and now Warren saw that the Japs were surging forward. Waves of them, following close behind mobile fortresses that were creeping up to that breached wall.

Those new contraptions were nearly two stories high, tremendous creations of steel that were half-tank and half-battering ram. Their two walls rose almost straight and came to a point in the front like a plow. Open in the back, they gave shelter to dozens of Japanese soldiers who were mounted on little platforms, pouring a hail of machine-gun fire through apertures in the steel plates.

But it was the front of those creeping fortresses that drew a gasp of horror and a bitter oath from the Triumvir's lips!

Strapped helplessly to the front of the steel plates on each of the oncoming tanks were the half-naked bodies of American

Now they had driven that enemy line back, fleeing in confusion!

160

women! Young girls who screamed in fright and stared with horror-widened eyes! Pinioned there to take the brunt of the fire, their death was certain unless the defenders gave way and surrendered.

For a moment the horror-smitten defenders held their fire—and in that moment the first of the mobile fortresses reached the breached wall, plowed the rubble out of its way, and was through the aperture. Now the Japanese machine-guns were enfilading the American ranks, were hosing death in every direction—and out from behind the open steel wall rushed dozens of armor-clad soldiers anxious to get their hands on the women who were huddled in the center of the quadrangle.

Andrew Warren's lips moved soundlessly as he hurled himself at a gleaming-eyed warrior who looked as if he had stepped out of a page of medieval Japanese history. This was the end. Now it would be only a few moments more and death would sweep over that crumbling fortress as completely as it had claimed the defenders of the Alamo of old....

Warren shot the fellow through the face, and turned to meet the doom that must claim him at any moment—and in that instant he glimpsed a plane that flew low over the fortress; glimpsed something that dropped out of it and hurtled downward. Directly in the path of one of those oncoming fortress-tanks that dark object landed, not more than fifty feet from Warren.

The Triumvir stared—and could hardly believe the evidence of his eyes. It was a body—the body of a man in an ornate Japanese uniform, with a round face that seemed to smile complacently even in death.

"Saigoni!" a startled howl rose from the ranks of the Japanese. "Prince Saigoni!"

Incredulously, they gathered around the body of their fallen leader, and then turned their eyes toward the sky from which it had come. Now the plane was circling again, and another body was dropping from it. But this time a parachute opened above the descending figure; and instead of being a corpse it was very much alive.

Too late they trained their guns upon it. Jimmy Christopher had already dropped inside the fortress—to be greeted by a tremendous cheer as the despairing defenders recognized him.

"Operator 5!" the magic name traveled from lip to lip like wildfire—and with it came new hope, new determination.

"Don't wait for them to come in!" Jimmy rallied them with a ringing challenge. "Drive them back before they get past the wall! We won't have to hold them much longer—Morelos and his Mexicans are coming to our aid! *Viva* Mexico!"

"Yeh, Morelos!" a wild cheer rose from hundreds of throats. *"Viva* Mexico!" they echoed him—and with ringing cheers they followed Operator 5 through that breached wall.

LIKE A spider Jimmy Christopher clambered up the front of one of those mobile fortresses the moment he reached it. From handhold to handhold he sped, cutting free the suspended girls—and then he was behind the steel shield, leading his men in a charge that swept everything before it. First one and then another of the war machines were captured, were turned around—and sent lumbering back into the ranks of the Japanese, with Americans manning the machine-guns now.

Those mobile fortresses so suddenly turned against them completed the panic of the disorganized Japanese. Their leader slain and hurled at them from the sky, their own weapons plowing through them and cutting them down, and those astounding Americans cheering for Mexico and for Morelos—it was too much for the Orientals. Quick to scent treachery, their officers hastily ordered a withdrawal; backed out of the shattered ruins that was Santa Fe and tried to reorganize their ranks on the plains beyond.

But now the Americans, their ranks mysteriously augmented as if the magic name of Operator 5 was able to raise men out of the ground, were taking the offensive. Pressing forward in captured tanks and trucks, they came on irresistibly. Before that berserk charge, the Orientals gave way again—fell back until their way was blocked by an enemy at their rear!

"Viva Mexico!" triumphant yells assailed them, and Avila Morelos' men came charging at them with blazing guns. *"Viva* Mexico! Back to Asia with the yellow invaders!"

Caught between deadly fire from the front and rear, the retreat of the Japanese became a rout. Jettisoning their ammunition and supplies, even deserting their tanks and ordnance, they fled for their lives—and many a yellow corpse dotted the barren plains of New Mexico before the last of the invaders reached the border, only to find fresh bands of Mexicans springing up on all sides to harry them and block their way.

AVILA MORELOS' revolution was won even before he

recrossed the border. Once he set foot on Mexican soil, his march to the capital was a triumphal procession. Toledaro did not even try to contest the way. As soon as he learned of the rout of his Japanese allies, he knew that his day was done, his fate sealed.

It is a matter of history how he tried to escape from Mexico City disguised as a *peon;* how he was recognized and hacked to pieces by the enraged citizens he had tried to enslave to Japan's Kasutosa. It has been estimated that there were close to two hundred thousand Japanese "farmers" and their "wives" in Mexico at the time of the American invasion—and less than twenty thousand of them managed to reach the West Coast and the sanctuary of vessels that carried them back to the Orient.

The part of friendship, that was sealed between President Avila Morelos and Triumvir Andrew Warren, is history, too.

"We will be good neighbors, *amigo,*" Morelos smiled his widest as he clasped the hand of Operator 5. "You have saved your United States—but you also have saved Mexico; and that we will not forget. If your country should need a friend, you will always have one below the Rio Grande."

If America needed a friend.... Jimmy Christopher's eyes stared out unseeingly toward the distant hills and his arm tightened around Diane's slim, fever-wasted form. Again he had performed a near-miracle; again he had snatched peace out of the very maw of war. Once more, thanks to that legion of unsung undercover heroes who had yielded their lives so that he might succeed, America had a breathing spell and could bend all her energies to the task of rebuilding and repairing.

There was peace today—but for how long? Until the nation was fully recovered; until it stood ready behind the security of an army and a navy that could defend it against the world, it would be like a traveler in a robber-infested wilderness. Constant vigilance was the price of safety—and to that legion of the dead Operator 5 owed a solemn obligation to see that this vigilance would never be relaxed!

AUTHOR'S NOTE: Even the desperate battle waged by Operator 5 and his aides on the Border, and its resultant success, did not afford America a very long breathing spell. As records of the time show, already an invasion—more weird than any the world had ever seen—was forming to capitalize the let-down prevalent in this country after the Japanese attack had failed. How Operator 5 met this new and fearful threat to his country is fully and dramatically told in the next installment.

POPULAR HERO PULPS AVAILABLE NOW:

THE SPIDER

- ❏ #1: The Spider Strikes — $13.95
- ❏ #2: The Wheel of Death — $13.95
- ❏ #3: Wings of the Black Death — $13.95
- ❏ #4: City of Flaming Shadows — $13.95
- ❏ #5: Empire of Doom! — $13.95
- ❏ #6: Citadel of Hell — $13.95
- ❏ #7: The Serpent of Destruction — $13.95
- ❏ #8: The Mad Horde — $13.95
- ❏ #9: Satan's Death Blast — $13.95
- ❏ #10: The Corpse Cargo — $13.95
- ❏ #11: Prince of the Red Looters — $13.95
- ❏ #12: Reign of the Silver Terror — $13.95
- ❏ #13: Builders of the Dark Empire — $13.95
- ❏ #14: Death's Crimson Juggernaut — $13.95
- ❏ #15: The Red Death Rain — $13.95
- ❏ #16: The City Destroyer — $13.95
- ❏ #17: The Pain Emperor — $13.95
- ❏ #18: The Flame Master — $13.95
- ❏ #19: Slaves of the Crime Master — $13.95
- ❏ #20: Reign of the Death Fiddler — $13.95
- ❏ #21: Hordes of the Red Butcher — $13.95
- ❏ #22: Dragon Lord of the Underworld — $13.95
- ❏ #23: Master of the Death-Madness — $13.95
- ❏ #24: King of the Red Killers — $13.95
- ❏ #25: Overlord of the Damned — $13.95
- ❏ #26: Death Reign of the Vampire King — $13.95
- ❏ #27: Emperor of the Yellow Death — $13.95
- ❏ #28: The Mayor of Hell — $13.95
- ❏ #29: Slaves of the Murder Syndicate — $13.95
- ❏ #30: Green Globes of Death — $13.95
- ❏ #31: The Cholera King — $13.95
- ❏ #32: Slaves of the Dragon — $13.95
- ❏ #33: Legions of Madness — $12.95
- ❏ #34: Laboratory of the Damned — $12.95
- ❏ #35: Satan's Sightless Legion — $12.95
- ❏ #36: The Coming of the Terror — $12.95
- ❏ #37: The Devil's Death-Dwarfs — $12.95
- ❏ #38: City of Dreadful Night — $12.95
- ❏ #39: Reign of the Snake Men — $12.95
- ❏ #40: Dictator of the Damned — $12.95
- ❏ #41: The Mill-Town Massacres — $12.95
- ❏ #42: Satan's Workshop — $12.95
- ❏ #43: Scourge of the Yellow Fangs — $12.95
- ❏ #44: The Devil's Pawnbroker — $12.95
- ❏ #45: Voyage of the Coffin Ship — $12.95
- ❏ #46: The Man Who Ruled in Hell — $13.95
- ❏ #47: Slaves of the Black Monarch — $13.95
- ❏ #48: Machineguns Over the White House — $13.95
- ❏ #49: The City That Dared Not Eat — $13.95
- ❏ #50: Master of the Flaming Horde — $13.95
- ❏ #51: Satan's Switchboard — $13.95
- ❏ #52: Legions of the Accursed Light — $13.95
- ❏ #53: The City of Lost Men — $13.95
- ❏ #54: The Grey Horde Creeps — $13.95
- ❏ #55: City of Whispering Death — $13.95
- ❏ #56: When Thousands Slept in Hell — $13.95
- ❏ #57: Satan's Shakles — $14.95
- ❏ #58: The Emperor From Hell — $14.95
- ❏ #59: The Devil's Candlesticks — $14.95
- ❏ #60: The City That Paid to Die — $14.95
- ❏ #61: The Spider at Bay — $14.95
- ❏ #62: Scourge of the Black Legions — $14.95
- ❏ #63: The Withering Death — $14.95
- ❏ #64: Claws of the Golden Dragon — $14.95
- ❏ #65: The Song of Death — $14.95
- ❏ #66: The Silver Death Reign — $14.95
- ❏ #67: Blight of the Blazing Eye — $14.95
- ❏ #68: King of the Fleshless Legion — $14.95
- ❏ #69: Rule of the Monster Men — $16.95
- ❏ #70: The Spider and the Slaves of Hell — $16.95
- ❏ #71: The Spider and the Fire God — $16.95
- ❏ #72: The Corpse Broker — $16.95
- ❏ #73: The Spider and the Eyeless Legion — $16.95
- ❏ *NEW:* #74: The Spider and the Faceless One — $16.95

THE WESTERN RAIDER

- ❏ #1: Guns of the Damned — $13.95
- ❏ #2: The Hawk Rides Back from Death — $13.95
- ❏ #3: Gun-Call for the Lost Legion — $13.95
- ❏ #4: The Law of Silver Trent — $13.95
- ❏ #5: The Gun-Prayer of Silver Trent — $13.95
- ❏ #6: Silver Trent Rides Alone — $13.95

CAPTAIN SATAN

- ❏ #1: The Mask of the Damned — $13.95
- ❏ #2: Parole for the Dead — $13.95
- ❏ #3: The Dead Man Express — $13.95
- ❏ #4: A Ghost Rides the Dawn — $13.95
- ❏ #5: The Ambassador From Hell — $13.95

DR. YEN SIN

- ❏ #1: Mystery of the Dragon's Shadow — $12.95
- ❏ #2: Mystery of the Golden Skull — $12.95
- ❏ #3: Mystery of the Singing Mummies — $12.95

THE MASKED MARKSMAN

- ❏ #1: Death Takes an Encore — $16.95

ACE G-MAN

- ❏ #1: The Suicide Squad Reports for Death — $14.95
- ❏ #2: Coffins for the Suicide Squad — $14.95
- ❏ #3: Shells for the Suicide Squad — $14.95